"Grace, listen to me, please," Jimmy said in a tight voice. "I'm sorry. I know I've been kind of cranky with you."

"Not just me."

"Well, everyone, you, and Mike. And okay, Barbara, too," he added quickly. "Let me make it up to you. We'll all go to a club tomorrow night. How's that?"

"But you can't dance," Grace reminded him.

"You and Mike can dance," Jimmy said. "I'd enjoy just watching you. Honest. I want you to be friends, anyway. My best buddy and my best girl."

Grace looked through the windshield, seeing Mike as he'd been in the attic. "I think it would be better to do something alone," she said urgently. "Just you and me."

"No, don't be silly! I want to make it up to both of you," Jimmy said. "It'll be fun. You'll see."

It was clear that he was anxious to please her; Grace's heart ached. She searched his face, wishing with all her soul that she could feel what she once felt. She was sure she loved him, but she was no longer sure whether she was *in* love with him.

GRACE OF THE WILD ROSE INN

JENNIFER ARMSTRONG

BANTAM BOOKS

New York • Toronto • London • Sydney • Auckland

RL 5.0, age 012 and up

GRACE OF THE WILD ROSE INN

A Bantam Book/December 1994

The Starfire logo is a registered trademark of Bantam Books,
a division of Bantam Doubleday Dell Publishing Group, Inc.
Registered in U.S. Patent and Trademark Office and elsewhere.

ISBN 0-553-29912-3

Published simultaneously in the United States and Canada

*Bantam Books are published by Bantam Books, a division of Bantam Doubleday
Dell Publishing Group, Inc. Its trademark, consisting of the words "Bantam
Books" and the portrayal of a rooster, is Registered in U.S. Patent and Trademark
Office and in other countries. Marca Registrada. Bantam Books, 1540 Broadway,
New York, New York 10036.*

PRINTED IN THE UNITED STATES OF AMERICA

OPM   0 9 8 7 6 5 4 3 2 1

GRACE OF THE WILD ROSE INN

1944

Chapter One

GRACE MACKENZIE FOLDED her arms across her chest. "All right. What's your bargain this time, Mr. Staines?" she asked the old fisherman on the opposite side of the bar.

"I have in my pocket two gas ration stamps." He waved the blue stamps at her. "Will that get me a beer or will it not? You look happy enough to agree to anything tonight."

Grace leaned across the countertop as the jukebox ratcheted a Frank Sinatra record into place. "We're running a hotel and restaurant here, Mr. Staines. I can't say I need the gas, but I could sure use any sugar or meat stamps you might happen to have."

"My sugar stamps?" The fisherman clapped his forehead. "You drive a hard bargain, Missy."

"She's a MacKenzie, and this is the Wild Rose Inn," said a middle-aged woman named Helen Diggory. "Do you think they could have run this establishment for three hundred years if they didn't know a thing or two about business?"

Laughing, Grace turned away from the bar and pulled on the beer tap. "Thanks for reminding him, Helen."

She set the foaming glass down in front of the old man and looked around the tavern. The oak beams of the ceiling were black with three centuries of pipe smoke, and the pewter tankards that lined the open shelves were burnished like silver. Across the wide room from her the door to the street opened and shut as regularly as the waves that lapped the tar-soaked pilings of the harbor. A gang of rowdy sailors on leave danced with local girls as though there were no tomorrow, and tourists and Marblehead patrons crowded around the tables. With the laughing, talking, and dance tunes it was almost deafening, but it was music to Grace's ears. She couldn't remember ever feeling happier.

"Sometimes it's hard to remember there's a war on," she confided to Mr. Staines. "I almost feel ashamed that business is so good."

"Well it's a fine thing to see the young people enjoying themselves," the leather-faced man said.

"Hey, Grace!" A red-haired young woman pushed through the crowd and threw herself against the bar. "Got a Coke for me?"

"Not drinking beer anymore, Barbie?" Mr. Staines asked.

"I've sworn not to drink another beer until we've licked the Germans." Barbara Baxter slapped the bar for

2

emphasis and struck a patriotic pose, one hand over her heart. "Not another drop."

Grace smiled at her friend. "You're safe making that oath. It looks like Hitler's a goner."

"You got that right, sister," a sailor put in as he leaned against the bar for a moment to catch his breath. "We'll have them whipped in no time, now."

"The invasion on D-Day sure broke Germany's back," a boy named Pete Marion said over his root beer. "Our soldiers are marching across France and kicking those damned Krauts right in their a—"

"Thank you, Pete!" Grace interrupted. "We know they're marching across France and we know just what they're kicking."

"Then Johnny comes marching home again," Barbara sang. She grinned at Grace. "Except for some boys who get home tonight."

A flush of elation raced over Grace's cheeks and left her blue eyes sparkling with happy tears. She put one hand to her face and laughed. "I still can't believe Jimmy's really going to be here, right here in the Wild Rose. Tonight. And he doesn't have to go back to France ever again."

"Planning a hero's welcome?" Mr. Staines asked.

Her eyes wet, Grace turned away and busied herself wiping down the bar with a towel. Jimmy Penworthy, her childhood sweetheart, was returning to Marblehead for good. After three years in the service he had done his duty by his country, and paid a heavy price for the honor, too. He had been counted among the thousands wounded on

3

the beaches of Normandy in June: he was coming home lame in one leg, but he was coming home and that was all that Grace cared about.

Ever since she could remember, Jimmy Penworthy had been the lighthouse of her existence. Older by five years, he had always been a hero to her, for many years like a wonderful big brother. He had defended her from stray dogs, taken her trick-or-treating when her own brother wouldn't, shown her how to swim and how to dig clams, carried her books when she'd broken her arm, and patiently taught her how to dance before her first formal.

And because the Penworthys and the MacKenzies were two of the oldest families in town, many of their neighbors had promoted their friendship as natural and inevitable. As Grace had matured, she and Jimmy found themselves trying out a new kind of relationship, but the war had put their growing love and their happy plans on hold. During three long yearning years of letters and secrets sent back and forth across the Atlantic, they had reached an understanding of what the future would bring for them both: a life together.

Grace felt the color rush to her cheeks as she thought of him walking through the door of the tavern and taking her in his arms. She pressed one hand to her stomach and drew a deep breath.

"He's a lucky boy, that's all I'll say," Mr. Staines said in a sentimental tone. He clucked his tongue as he looked at Grace. "You're going to make a beautiful bride."

"Oh, I . . ." Grace's throat closed on her words. Her

heart pounded wildly at the word "bride," and she felt breathless with excitement.

"Hey, don't marry her off too fast," Barbara snorted as the jukebox switched to a swing tune and several couples began to jitterbug. "There hasn't been any official announcement."

Another sailor washed up against the bar. "How about a dance?" he asked Grace.

She rang a customer's check into the cash register. "No, thanks."

Barbara gave the fellow a sizing-up. "According to this geezer she's taken, but I'm not."

"Let's go, then," the sailor said, grabbing Barbara's hand.

"That Barbara, she's a corker," Pete said, wide-eyed with admiration. "Even with sixteen girls for every guy, she can get a dance."

Grace laughed. "And she's right about one thing. Jimmy hasn't even asked me to marry him. Maybe he won't. As you say, there are sixteen girls for every guy, these days. Maybe he'll want to take his pick."

"Nonsense," Mr. Staines said. He took a long pull on his beer and wiped the foam from his upper lip. "Best match for both of you. Two of the oldest families in town —it's about time you were hitched up."

"Hear, hear," Pete agreed smiling, raising his glass.

Grace gave Pete a wry glance and then made a quick check of the room. Everyone was happy, everyone content. The tavern of the Wild Rose Inn filled up every night, summer, fall, winter, and spring, and there was never a complaint heard: the war had put everyone in a sacrificing, generous mood, and tempers actually improved as the war worsened.

"Ah, Grace, you're a marvel," a retired merchant named Wiggins said. "You run this place like a ship."

"Well, it's all well and good for her to be running the Wild Rose while her dad and brother are off fighting the Japs in the Pacific," another old codger warned.

"She's doing a fine job of it, too," Mr. Staines put in, smiling indulgently. "And your mother so wrapped up in her poetry."

"My mother writes novels," Grace corrected him.

"But Grace will have to get used to playing second fiddle once she and Jimmy do settle down," the other man continued.

"Not Grace," Barbara said, suddenly bursting into their midst. "She's in the habit of command now. Oh, give me a Coke, Gracie, I'm dying."

Grace shrugged. "Who knows," she said in an aside to her friend. "Maybe if they'd put me in charge of the Third Army this war would have been over by now."

Barbara crooked her finger at Grace, and the two girls put their heads together as the men talked war amongst themselves in a cozy, home-front general sort of way.

"Don't they make you want to do something shocking?" Barbara whispered.

"Like what?" Grace asked.

"Like dance naked on the bar singing 'Home on the Range.'"

6

Grace let out a scream of laughter. "You're terrible!" she gasped, her eyes sparkling. "Those salty old fishermen would be scandalized if I sang a *cowboy* song."

Barbara choked on her soda. "Oh, you're a bad girl, Grace MacKenzie. Why I should—"

The telephone behind the bar rang, and Grace snatched it up, her pulse beating wildly in the hollow of her throat. "Hello?"

"Grace MacKenzie? Is that you? This is Loretta Dugget over in Swampscott. I thought you'd like to know the bus from Boston just left and I can confirm that that sweet Jimmy Penworthy's on it. Sitting right in front like the hero he is. Saw him with my very own eyes."

Grace pressed one hand to her cheek. She felt almost faint. "Thank you, Mrs. Dugget."

"The bus oughtta be there in half an hour."

"Thank you," Grace repeated in a whisper.

Trembling slightly, she replaced the telephone in its cradle and turned around. Everyone at the bar was watching her expectantly, every face beaming with goodwill and expectation.

"Well?" Barbara demanded.

"That was Mrs. Dugget," Grace began.

Barbara pulled a face. "The old gossip. What particular tidbit of fascinating news did she have?"

"The bus just left Swampscott and Jimmy's on it," Grace said with mounting excitement. "He's on his way and he'll be here in half an hour!"

Mr. Staines let out a shout. "Did you hear that, everyone? Jimmy Penworthy's on his way!"

There was a general chorus of approval and even some applause. Everyone knew Jimmy, and they were proud of their hometown hero.

"They say he took out a German machine-gun nest single-handed," one man said to his neighbor.

"Saved a buddy's life, too, is what I heard, even though he was wounded himself."

"It's boys like that who are going to win this war for us. That's what makes this country great."

"The GIs deserve nothing but the best. Royal treatment, all the way."

"I'd be proud to call that boy son."

Grace struggled out of her apron and ducked under the flap at the end of the bar. "You've got to help me," she begged her friend. "I look like something that fell out of a herring net. Come on."

"Don't you go helping yourselves at those taps, now," Barbara warned the men.

"I'll keep an eye on them," Mr. Staines promised.

Grace and Barbara grabbed hands and dodged their way through the crowd, side-stepping dancers and folks standing together talking over their drinks in the low-ceilinged room. The old tavern, built in the late sixteen-hundreds, was all that was left of the original Wild Rose Inn: a fire had destroyed the rambling additions of two centuries in 1898. But the inn had grown again over the years since then, and was as rambling and comfortable as ever. Grace led the way down a carpeted hall to the bright kitchen.

"Let me just get someone to cover for me in the bar," she told her friend quickly.

"Where's your mother?" Barbara asked.

"Boston," Grace said, turning the corner.

Accented voices reached them in the hallway.

"Why shouldn't I feed my child treats? Didn't he have enough hunger in Germany?"

"But he's going to get fat, Rachel."

"So who cares if he's fat? He says he's hungry and I'll feed him."

Grace stuck her head around the door. A tall, gaunt man stood at the kitchen table, arguing with the tiny, dark-haired woman peeling potatoes across from him. David and Rachel Teitelbaum, refugees from Germany, worked as hard as two couples in spite of the hardships they had suffered. Under the table six-year-old Nathan was provisioning a fort with the food his mother was handing him.

"David, can you man the bar?" Grace asked, smiling at the family. "I've got to run upstairs and change my clothes."

David and Rachel immediately broke off their bickering. They maintained a constant low-level argument with a total absence of rancor, and could halt in mid-squabble and then resume as easily as breathing. They both smiled at Grace.

"You already look like a movie star," Rachel said, taking the opportunity to slip Nathan a handful of cookies.

9

Grace laughed. "Sure, like Humphrey Bogart, maybe."

"Grace, I'm making a fort," Nathan called from under the table. "Do you want to come in?"

"Not right now, sweetie. But I'll visit you later," Grace said, giving the Teitelbaums an airy wave.

"They're the most adorable couple," Barbara said with a laugh as Grace led the way to the stairs. "That was the kindest thing you ever did, hiring them."

"They're excellent workers," Grace said. Their shoes clattered on the wooden steps, and their shadows raced up the stairs with them.

" 'Excellent workers,' you old softy," Barbara teased her.

Grace laughed and put her shoulder to the door of her bedroom under the eaves of the old tavern. "They are excellent workers. I refuse to be accused of sentimentality when it comes to this business."

"Okay, Grace. Whatever you say. You're as tough as an Army boot."

Smiling, Grace turned her back on her friend. "Undo me, will you?"

She sighed happily as Barbara undid the row of buttons on her dress. All around the room were the girlish mementos of her school days: road signs filched from town, posters for school plays and victory dances, a "Buy US War Bonds" sign with Uncle Sam's stern face and pointing finger. Her teddy bear, the tassel from her graduation cap, Jimmy's old varsity jacket hanging in a place of honor over the bed: these things surrounded her with a powerful sense of security and joy.

"I have wonderful news," Grace said. "We got a letter from my brother today. He doesn't want to run the inn when he gets out of the Navy. He wants to go to Hollywood and become a director for one of the big studios."

Barbara grabbed Grace's shoulders and spun her around. Her green eyes were wide with jubilation. "So you'll get to run the place yourself?"

"It's mine if I want it," Grace said.

"And you want it! Oh, Grace! You'll be the boss for good! You always hoped it would happen this way!"

Grace laughed and shrugged out of her cotton dress. "I figured at most I'd be Mark's partner when Dad retired, but now I feel like I could fly into the air, I'm so happy. Everything I ever wanted is mine tonight. The Wild Rose and Jimmy."

"You're one lucky stiff." Barbara gave Grace a hug.

Grace hugged her friend back. "Help me with my seams, would you?"

She hopped up onto a chair, and Barbara took a black eyebrow pencil from the dressing table.

"Hike up your slip," Barbara said, bracing herself to draw stocking seams on the backs of Grace's legs. Music beat faintly through the floorboards from the tavern below, and through the open window came the scent of the ocean. Barbara drew the pencil up the back of Grace's knee.

Grace shrieked. "That tickles!"

"You're just giddy, that's all. Hold still. I hope having

11

Jimmy back isn't going to make you go all girly and gooey on me."

"Of course not, don't worry," Grace said, craning around to look down at the top of her friend's head. The center part in Barbara's red hair was white and straight, as neat and uncompromising as Barbara herself. The girls had only become friends in the last year, although they had known each other in school. Secretly, Grace had always been somewhat in awe of the older, strong-minded, fast-talking Barbara. Once they had both taken part-time jobs at the local fish factory, however, they had spent more and more time together, and Grace knew what a heart of gold her friend had. Now they were almost inseparable. Grace squelched a nervous twinge at how Jimmy would react to their friendship: "a real piece of work" was how he had once jokingly referred to Barbara Baxter. But Grace was confident he'd come to love and value Barbara as much as Grace herself did, once he got to know her.

"I just don't want you to forget about me when your sweetie pie comes home," Barbara said, still concentrating on her task.

"Are you out of your mind?" Grace demanded. She hopped down off the chair and gave her friend a hug. "How could I get along without you?"

Barbara rolled her eyes and tossed the pencil back on the dressing table. "Well, once the war is over, we'll be able to get nylons again and you won't need me to draw seams for you."

"Oh, you're right. I guess I won't need you for anything at all," Grace said, opening her closet. She glanced over her shoulder and gave Barbara a wink.

Barbara grabbed a hairbrush and brandished it at Grace. "Why I oughtta . . ."

There was a burst of music from downstairs and Grace felt a sudden wild leap in her heart. She paused as she buckled the belt of her dress.

"He'll be here any minute," she said in a tone of amazement.

The wry expression on Barbara's face melted into tenderness. She stepped forward and gave Grace a kiss on the cheek. "Go on downstairs. You look wonderful. He'll think he's in heaven when he sees what an angel you are."

They held hands for a moment. Grace's heart was so full she thought she would cry. "I'm so happy."

"I know," Barbara said. "You deserve it, too."

With a breathless laugh, Grace smoothed her dress down and hurried to the door. Voices and laughter from the tavern reached them as they ran down the stairs, and the two girls reentered the tavern just as a nearby air-raid siren went off.

"Oh, not again!" someone groaned.

"I'm so sick of blackouts," another man grumbled. "Those Germans are too busy running for cover to bomb us."

With matter-of-fact efficiency everyone pulled down the blackout shades at the windows and switched off the lights. Grace felt her way through the darkness to the bar, and heard David Teitelbaum muttering under his breath.

"Probably just that foolish old Mr. Bowman," David

said. "The man is blind as a bat. Who made him air-raid warden?"

There were muffled whispers, and a girl shrieked suddenly and lapsed into giggles. Over the voices of sailors singing "Ask What the Boys in the Back Room Will Have," Grace could hear her heart pounding. In the darkness, the image of Jimmy's face was as bright as a candle to her eyes. Her fingers sought the locket at her throat, and she put it to her lips to kiss the heart with his picture in it. A few more minutes of waiting and he'd be home to stay. All the dreams that had filled her nights for the last three years were about to come true at last. She could hear Mrs. Penworthy, Jimmy's widowed mother, who must have just arrived, whispering breathlessly to a companion.

The all clear finally sounded, and someone flicked a light switch. For a moment Grace stood blinking against the dazzle. She could hear the outside door open, and the room went silent.

And when she opened her eyes fully, Jimmy was standing in front of her, his hat at an angle, his coat over his shoulder. Grace stared at him, her heart soaring.

"Grace," he whispered.

He stepped forward and swept her into his arms.

Chapter Two

A ROUSING CHEER went up and echoed off the old tavern walls, as though the house itself roared its approval. Grace felt herself lifted right off her toes as Jimmy pulled her close, and then, for a moment, the sounds of the crowd disappeared.

"I've been dreaming of this moment," he whispered in her ear. He kissed her throat and pressed his face into her shoulder.

"Me, too," she breathed. She tipped her head back and looked up into his blue eyes. To her surprise there were lines at the corners that hadn't been there three years ago, and a deep furrow between his brows, and he had filled out through the shoulders. He looked much more changed than she had expected, but he was still Jimmy Penworthy. And he was holding her in his arms. He smiled from ear to ear and bent to kiss her again, and Grace felt her heart knock against her ribs.

Gradually, they became aware of stomping feet and

15

rhythmic clapping, and there were catcalls and laughter. At once Grace stepped back. She pressed both hands against her flushed face.

"Now that's what I call a hero's welcome!" someone shouted.

"What a touching scene," a nearby woman said with a sigh.

"Welcome home, Jim!" Mr. Staines called out.

Jimmy caught sight of his mother, standing with both hands clasped to her heart and a look of absolute joy on her face. A broad smile lit Jimmy's features. "Ma!" He crossed to her and picked up the buxom woman in a big bear hug.

"Oh, Jimmy!" she shrieked, crying and laughing at the same time. "Oh, my darling boy!"

There was another round of greetings, with dozens of well-wishers shaking Jimmy's hand and clapping him on the back. Grace could hardly take her eyes off him, hardly dared look away for fear that he'd be gone when she looked for him again. But at last another green uniform caught her attention. The crowd parted, and she noticed the young man who had come into the Wild Rose behind Jimmy. He stood at his ease, a faded army duffel slung over one shoulder, watching the reunion with a good-natured smile. Then he turned and their eyes met, and Grace felt a strange jolt of recognition.

"Hello," Grace said uncertainly. She held out her hand. "Have we met? Did you come with Jim?"

He swung his duffel down onto the floor with a thump and shook her hand. "Mike Holmquist."

"Oh! You're Mike!" Grace gripped his hand with both of hers, and Jimmy turned around eagerly.

"Didn't I tell you I wrote her all about you, Mike?" Jimmy said as he put one arm across Grace's shoulder.

Mike smiled again. His eyes were warm brown and wrinkled as Jimmy's were by stress and war. "I've heard all about you too, Grace," he said.

"I hope you aren't already bored with me," Grace replied with a laugh. She couldn't stop smiling at him. "But I sure feel like I've known you for at least two years already."

She sized him up, remembering the letters in which Jimmy had written of his buddy Mike, the medic, and of their other pal, Vic, who fell on the beach at Normandy. Mike had a kind face and an easy, unassuming manner, and Grace felt an instant closeness with Jimmy's friend.

"Got a bunk for him here, honey?" Jimmy asked, giving her shoulder a squeeze.

"Of course." She grimaced as the noise suddenly crescendoed around them and a swing tune blasted from the jukebox. "If you don't mind staying in this madhouse," she shouted at Mike.

"After a battlefield nothing seems noisy anymore," he insisted, pushing his cap back over his blond crew cut. "I've taken naps in more noise than this."

"Be back in a second, Grace," Jimmy said. He turned away, his hand lifted in a wave as he moved off.

Grace felt a surge of happiness and well-being so strong that she almost felt like crying. She looked around her at the familiar faces of her neighbors and friends. Al-

17

most everyone dear to her was there, Penworthys and Bowmans and Carters and Bulls. Everyone wanted to shake Jimmy's hand, and he was making the rounds with a smile. He limped noticeably as he moved through the crowd, but when someone pointed to his leg he made an airy gesture with one hand.

"Yeah, I got shot up pretty good, but I took out plenty of Krauts before they took me out of action," he said loudly.

Grace felt sudden tears flood her eyes. She wiped them away with the back of her hand.

"Are you all right?" Mike asked.

"Oh, what a sentimental fool I am," she laughed. Grace looked up at Mike, sniffing and smiling at the same time. She took a handkerchief from her pocket and dabbed her eyes. "I'm so glad he's back, and he looks fine. There's nothing for me to cry about."

"I always knew he was a lucky guy to have someone miss him so much," Mike told her. "You look like you've been holding your breath."

Grace slipped her arm through his and led him to the bar. "Not exactly," she replied. "Sometimes I've gone for five minutes at a time without thinking of him."

"Ah, don't you believe her," David Teitelbaum said, solemnly shaking Mike's hand. "She has been so loyal and brave, it warms my heart to see such a girl."

Mike leaned his elbows on the bar. "Well, the long struggle to be stalwart is over. You can turn to mush now."

"Thanks," Grace said, laughing. "I'm so glad you

came with Jimmy. I know we're all going to be best friends."

"I hope so, too." Mike let out a contented sigh.

"Thirsty?" Grace took a glass and filled it with beer. "Here. For soldiers, the first beer is always free. And since you're Jimmy's friend, they'll all be the first beer."

"That sounds good to me."

"Hey, honey," Jimmy said, joining them at the bar and kissing Grace on the cheek.

She blushed delightedly, and David handed another beer across the bar for Jimmy. "Everyone's so happy to see you," she said, her eyes shining.

"Well, you can't blame them, I guess," Jimmy said with a shrug. "Small towns don't get a lot of 'Hail the Conquering Hero' stuff. Thanks," he added, raising his glass to her.

Mike was grinning. "Don't let it go to your head, Penworthy. The novelty will wear off soon enough."

Jimmy made a fist and waved it in front of his buddy's nose, but he was laughing. "Well, that's all I want. Everything back to normal. Pick up right where I left off, that's the only thing on my agenda."

He looked at Grace as he spoke, and she felt another flush of happiness color her cheeks. "That sounds perfect to me, too," she whispered.

Jimmy winked at her and took a sip of his beer. "Say, where's your mother? I thought for sure she'd want to say hi to me."

"Of course she did, but she's been in Boston for two days," Grace told him. "She got a serious nibble on her book from one of the big publishers and had to be there for some meetings. She'll be back late tonight."

Jimmy sent a wry glance Mike's way. "Her mother is a lady novelist," he explained. "Can you beat that? Mr. MacKenzie even eggs her on."

"She sounds impressive," Mike said, looking at Grace.

She nodded. "I'm so proud of her. I'm positive she'll sell the book this time. Just last—"

"Say, Grace," Jimmy interrupted. He gestured with his beer glass. "Isn't that Miss Bossy Barbara Baxter over there?"

Grace landed a playful punch on Jimmy's arm. "She's not so bossy. And you know she's my friend now. I wrote you all about the girls at the fish factory."

"The fish girls." Jimmy laughed. "That's rich."

Grace waved to Barbara, who nodded and made her way through the crowd. "I want you to be nice to her," Grace told Jimmy in an undertone as her friend approached.

"Hail glorious Caesar we salute you," Barbara said as she joined them. She saluted Jimmy with a sardonic smile. "Welcome home."

Jimmy shook her hand. "Hey, Barbara. Nice to see you. This is my buddy, Mike Holmquist."

Grace watched anxiously as Jimmy and Barbara and Mike made introductions and parried the usual small talk back and forth. She glanced up at Jimmy, uncertain whether in fact he and Barbara would get along.

"Where are you from, Mike?" Barbara asked. "You sound like a flatlander to me."

He grinned. "I thought a couple years in the Army would've rubbed that off," he said, shaking his head. "I guess you can take the boy off the prairie, but you can't take the . . ."

"Prairie off the boy," Barbara finished.

Jimmy took Grace's arm and led the way to a table where they sat, hand in hand. "I like your friend," Grace told him happily. "He seems like a terrific guy."

"He's the best," Jimmy agreed. His gaze wandered around the crowded tavern and followed David and Rachel Teitelbaum busily serving drinks. "Are those your refugees?"

"I wouldn't exactly call them 'my refugees,'" Grace said. "They are my friends, though."

Jimmy looked at her with a beaming smile and stroked her cheek with one finger. "You are completely adorable, you know that? Such an angel of mercy."

Grace turned her face into his hand and kissed his palm. "I'm nothing special," she murmured.

"I'll be the judge of that." He waggled his eyebrows up and down, and Grace laughed.

"I had a vision when I was shot," Jimmy went on in a mock-dramatic tone. "This vision came to me that I would know all and see all. And I know that you are my guardian angel, and that of all the girls in the world—"

"Knock it off, you screwball!" Grace laughed again and twined her fingers through his. "Of all the guys in the world you are definitely the most—"

21

"In love with you," he interrupted.

Grace felt her breath catch in her throat, and for a moment, she couldn't speak. Dance music swelled joyfully around them, leaving the two of them in an island of peace and contentment.

"Are you the hero?" came a childish voice.

Jimmy broke from Grace's gaze and looked down at Nathan. "Well, Buster. Who are you?"

"This is Nathan Teitelbaum," Grace said, smoothing the boy's hair fondly. "And he'll be happy to tell you that he's six years old."

"Six and one half. Did you kill many Nazis?" Nathan asked solemnly.

Jimmy leaned his elbows on his knees and brought his face down to Nathan's level. "I sure did," he boasted.

While a wide-eyed Nathan listened to Jimmy recount his story, Grace watched Jimmy's face.

"There we were," Jimmy began. "It was dark, early in the morning. The weather had been terrible for days, and the waves in the English Channel were as high as the gunnels of our ships. We knew the beaches of France were just ahead of us in the dark, and that those beaches were crawling with German soldiers. They were bunkered in, machine-gun nests covering the coast for miles in both directions. But we had to go in. We knew it was our destiny."

A few people pulled their chairs closer, and in a small circle around Jimmy, voices dropped and went silent.

"We'd been waiting for the signal for invasion for

days, back in England. The brass were trying to juggle tides, the moon, and the weather and come up with a perfect crossing, but all we had was one lousy day after another. We all knew the word was coming, but we weren't sure when. So all those hundreds of thousands of men had nothing to do but wait and wonder when we'd have to face those guns."

Grace noticed Mike draw near. His eyes were downcast, and he fingered the dog tag at his throat like a talisman as Jimmy spoke.

Jimmy took a deep breath. "So the signal came, and suddenly time sped up. Before you knew what had happened, there we were, on the boats, getting nearer and nearer to France. Nearer to the Germans. Wondering when they'd see us and start shelling."

"Weren't you scared?" Nathan asked.

"No time to be scared," Jimmy replied. "My men were looking to me, and there's no time for a leader to be scared. Suddenly the firing started and we got the order to go over the side. The flak jackets we had on got soaked, and at first I thought I'd drown. But then I thought about my men and my duty to lead them onto the beach."

"Good for you, son," an elderly man said in a quivering voice. "God bless you."

Jimmy seemed not to hear. He narrowed his eyes and gripped his hands together. "We were sitting ducks in the water, too, slogging through, carrying our gear and our weapons, and the Krauts just sitting up there in those—those damn machine-gun nests picking us off like fish in a barrel. And men were falling—I bumped into a guy in the

23

water, and he rolled under, and then we were on the beach, and trying to fire even though we couldn't see." Jimmy took a harsh breath as Mike put one hand on his shoulder. "And there was that emplacement up over the beach where we had the bad luck to wash up, and my men and I had to take it. Mike and Vic and I were hunkered down behind a boulder, and I told Vic to wait for my signal and then we'd go, but he didn't wait!"

Jimmy's voice rose sharply. He sat back in his chair and seemed to collect himself. Grace took his hand and held it tightly. Her heart was pounding, and under the skin of his wrist she felt his pulse beating hard and fast.

"What happened to Vic?" Nathan asked.

"Vic got hit," Jimmy said. He pushed his chair back abruptly. "Maybe if he'd listened to me he wouldn't have. Excuse me, folks."

He pushed his way, limping, through the crowd. Grace watched his retreat, her eyes stinging. A sympathetic murmur of voices rippled through the room.

Nathan turned to Grace with a puzzled frown. "Vic got hit?"

"That means he got shot. He was killed," she said quietly. "And Jimmy got hurt trying to help him, and he feels pretty sad about his friend."

She looked up at Mike as she spoke. He was staring off in the direction that Jimmy had gone.

"But Jimmy took those Germans out," a voice in the crowd muttered. Rachel tut-tutted over Nathan and led him away, whispering about bedtime.

Grace still watched Mike. His face was filled with

pain, and she remembered that of course, Vic had been Mike's buddy, too. Her heart went out to him.

"Have a seat," she offered, pulling out a chair for him.

"Thanks."

He sat, still frowning. He was folding and unfolding his cloth cap as he stared into space. The jukebox started up again as the people in the bar slowly shed their somber mood.

"You must miss Vic, too," Grace said, watching Mike's hands.

"I miss a lot of the guys," Mike replied. "A lot of good men . . ."

Grace leaned forward. "Did Jimmy save your life that day?" Grace asked. "His letters—I know he didn't like to say, but I got the feeling there was something he didn't want to tell me. He was too modest to say so, maybe."

Slowly Mike turned his eyes on her. He didn't answer right away, and Grace waited for him to confirm what she had guessed. Instead, he focused on something behind her. Grace turned to see Jimmy limping back to the table.

"Hey, honey," he said, sitting down again with a sheepish smile. "Sorry, I didn't mean to get so worked up just now. But once a guy gets started on war stories . . ."

"Don't apologize." She put her hand in his.

"Well, enough gloom and doom, huh?" Jimmy nodded toward the jukebox. "How about a dance with my best girl?"

25

"Your leg!" Grace and Mike both spoke at the same time.

Jimmy arched his eyebrows. "It's nice to know you both care so much about my gimpy leg," he said, laughing.

"You know it's still healing," Mike said.

"Okay, doc." Jimmy sat back in his chair, one arm across the back of Grace's. "But tomorrow night, we're going out on the town." He spoke with the authority of a man accustomed to giving orders.

Grace made a rueful face. "Tomorrow night your mother is making you a special dinner. She's been planning it ever since she knew you'd be coming home and you can't disappoint her."

He frowned, the crease between his brows deepening. "Oh, all right. So we'll go to the beach tomorrow afternoon."

Grace shook her head. "I wish I could," she began reluctantly. "But I'll be working at the fish factory."

"Hey, it's a special occasion, isn't it?" Jimmy asked. "They'll understand. Help out a GI."

"They're trying to help all the GI's," Grace said, shifting uncomfortably on her chair. "My boss is really serious about not shirking your duty."

"Can't you call in sick or something?" Jimmy demanded.

"Jimmy!" Grace blushed and sent an embarrassed glance at Mike.

Barbara set a glass of soda on the table and pulled out a chair for herself. "Don't get up, fellas," she said.

Mike rose automatically, but Jimmy shrugged and didn't bother. "Go ahead and call in sick tomorrow," he urged Grace. "It's not like it's such an important job."

"Being an assistant bookkeeper is important," Barbara said, glancing from Grace to Jimmy.

"Well, maybe it is," Jimmy said. "But Grace doesn't have to do the job anymore. The fellas are coming home from overseas. You girls have only had to work because the men weren't here. Now it's time to give up the job for a GI."

Grace stared down into her lap. She could feel the color in her cheeks, and she knew Barbara was looking at her. She was rather taken aback by Jimmy's attitude.

"And anyway, once we're married, you won't have to work," Jimmy added with an air of having settled everything. "Not my girl."

Grace forced a breezy laugh. "But I like it, Jimmy. Just you try to stop me from working. And when my dad decides to retire, I'll have this place to run."

He laughed, too, and touched the tip of her nose with one finger. "We'll see about that."

Barbara stood up abruptly. "Let's get the boys some beer, Grace!" she suggested in a bright, cheerful voice. She took Grace's hand and dragged her out of her chair.

"Be right back!" Barbara called, waving at Jimmy and Mike over her shoulder.

"What's wrong?" Grace asked, sending her friend a doubtful look.

Barbara edged her way to the bar, and held up two fingers to David Teitelbaum. Then she leaned on one elbow and looked long and hard at Grace. Grace waited, feeling slightly piqued.

"Well, are you going to come clean?" Grace asked at last.

"I didn't want to spoil this nice homecoming," Barbara said at last.

"I don't know what you mean."

Barbara smiled with one side of her mouth. "Just don't be so happy to have him home that you let him boss you around."

"Oh, don't be silly," Grace scoffed. She picked up the beers and gave Barbara a confident smile. "He would never boss me around."

"Grace." David, who had been listening, broke in. "I beg your pardon, but I would like to say one thing."

The girls turned to look at him. David shook his head, his eyes sober and dark. "A man wants respect. A woman should remember that."

"Respect!" Barbara let out an unladylike snort and threw her hands into the air. "If he deserves it, that's fine with me."

Grace drew herself a fraction away from her friend. Barbara had never struck her before as quite so harsh and opinionated. With a sidelong glance at Barbara, Grace wondered if Jimmy was right to call her Miss Bossy. After all, there was absolutely nothing wrong with being glad to have Jimmy home. And he did deserve special treatment after what he'd been through. He was a decorated war hero, wounded in the service of his country. That deserved plenty of respect.

And besides he was accustomed to giving orders. It was only natural that he would be in the habit of making decisions. But that would wear off now that he was out of the service, she reasoned.

She looked for him in the crowd. Mike and Jimmy had their heads together across the table, talking and tracing figures on the tablecloth with their fingers. Then Jimmy looked up and met Grace's eyes across the tavern. He smiled, and Grace was sure it was worth any price.

Chapter Three

GRACE WAS AWAKENED early the next morning when her mother shook her by the shoulder. She opened her eyes and then shut them again with a groan, pulling the pillow over her face.

"Come on, sleepyhead," Hope MacKenzie said, yanking the pillow away. "Rise and shine."

"I'll rise, but I don't think I can shine," Grace said, dragging herself upright. She squinted against the pale light that flooded the diamond-paned window and made an aura around its edges. Then she stretched hugely. "How was your meeting with the publisher, Mom?"

Mrs. MacKenzie leaned against the windowsill with her long, dark hair pulled over her shoulder and swung one leg back against the wall. "Scale of one to seventy-two, it was maybe a six."

"You're kidding!" Grace regarded her mother, whose face was in shadow against the window. "They don't want your novel?"

"Well, let's just say they were very polite. Very encouraging. They thought I should write about something besides corrupt businessmen. Something more 'womanly' I think they said. Something with romance."

Grace sighed and wrapped her arms around her knees. She was almost in awe of her mother, of her utter disregard for what others thought she should do and her stubborn insistence on following her heart's desire in spite of all opposition. Grace wished she herself could be as confident as her mother was.

"Did they say they'd think about it, at least?"

Mrs. MacKenzie let out a wry laugh and pushed herself away from the window. "Oh, naturally. In the meantime, maybe I'll start something new, something about the romance of waiting for your husband to come home from the war. But let's get off the subject," she said, sitting on the bed beside Grace. "Tell me all about Jimmy."

Grace flopped back against her pillow and smiled dreamily at the Marblehead High School pennant tacked to the wall above her desk. "It was so wonderful."

"You can do better than that," her mother prompted. She grinned. "Wonderful? Please."

"Fabulous, glorious, fantastic," Grace said, tossing her bedraggled old teddy bear at her mother. "He came in like the conquering hero that he is, everyone thrilled to see him, especially me, and now at last we can take up just where we left off."

Mrs. MacKenzie made the teddy bear dance on her lap for a moment and then sent Grace a questioning glance. "You've been saying that since he left. What are you going to do, pretend the last three years didn't exist?"

"Mother." Grace winced. "Of course not. But after all, nothing's really changed."

Her mother danced the teddy bear for another moment and then tossed it across the room into a chair. "Except that you're not a child anymore. Children don't run hotels the way you do."

"Well, of course I'm not a child! I know time didn't stand still, but I'm still me and he's still Jimmy. End of story." She threw herself back against the pillows again and clasped her hands behind her head.

Her mother combed her fingers through her long hair while she regarded Grace. She was only sixteen years older than her daughter, and her face was still young and beautiful. But there was a deep mystery in her brown eyes that always convinced Grace that her mother was as wise as the ancients. Now Grace shifted uncertainly under Mrs. MacKenzie's steady gaze. She remembered those uneasy moments the previous night when Jimmy had been irritable and impatient and curt; she looked down to fiddle with the red piping on her pajama top.

"We still love each other and that's what really counts," she muttered.

"Maybe you're right," Mrs. MacKenzie said. She stood up and went to the window. "Maybe war doesn't change men, after all. Maybe it just makes them more of what they were to begin with."

Grace looked at her mother's straight back. "Are you thinking about Dad? He'll never change, I'm sure of that."

"I'm sure of that, too."

Pity and fear suddenly crowded into Grace's heart; she pictured her father and brother still in the war, still in danger. She knew her mother ached with anxiety over her men, and Grace almost felt ashamed for her own happiness and relief. She crossed to the window and rested her chin on her mother's shoulder so that they both looked out the window onto the awakening street.

Below them the paper boy threw the morning edition of the newspaper onto doorsteps. Both women averted their eyes: neither of them liked to read the war news first thing in the morning. It was an unspoken agreement between them. For a few minutes at the start of every day, they would pretend the world was not at war, and that life everywhere was as peaceful as Marblehead. They would pretend that the town was not just populated by women, old men, and boys, that the men were nearby and on their way home in a few minutes.

"Jimmy brought a friend home with him," Grace said to distract her mother from her worries. "One of his buddies, Mike Holmquist. I put him in number seventeen."

"Wonderful," Mrs. MacKenzie said in a distant voice.

"You'll like him, too," Grace went on with a quick glance at her mother's profile. "He's sweet and quiet and friendly."

Mrs. MacKenzie reached up and put one hand to Grace's cheek. "Wonderful, sweetheart. I look forward to meeting him."

Grace turned away and began to dress. From time to time she cast a look or a comment to her mother, but the

33

older woman was standing motionless at the window, gazing at the harbor. In that somber mood, Grace knew, her mother was unreachable. Hope MacKenzie was a woman of violent passions and strong opinions and never tried to pass off her fears with a smile as Grace did. Grace planted a kiss on her mother's pale cheek and slipped out of her bedroom to get the workday started.

As she walked down the hallway, Grace heard the comfortable, cozy sounds of the house as it stirred. Her footsteps were muffled by worn blue carpet, and sunlight fell in through the windows in one yellow oblong after another. Grace passed silently through the squares of light and shadow, and then took the stairs down to the kitchen, following the voice of the radio.

Rachel was tying on an apron as Grace entered, and Sarah Quinn, a war widow who cooked for them, was checking over a brown bowl filled with eggs.

"Morning." Grace glanced at the small eggs. "Where did we get these?"

"Mrs. Furness," Sarah told her in a skeptical voice. "Pretty measly-looking eggs. Those hens of hers must not be eating much lately."

Grace laughed. "They got into my garden the other day and made mincemeat of my beans and scratched dirt all over the lettuce."

"I'd like to make mincemeat out of them," Rachel said as she measured coffee into a pot. "I'd love a nice stewed chicken for Nathan."

Grace and Sarah shared a smile. "Nathan gets fatter

and David gets leaner," Sarah observed in her wry fashion. "I wonder how that happens?"

"My David worries too much," Rachel said. "All the time he worries. I worry too, so many of our friends in Germany we'll never hear from again. But he can't be thankful we're here in America!"

David, coming in at that moment, shut the door carefully behind him. He drew himself up to his full height, his lean, bent frame straightening like a folding ruler. "I am thankful every moment I breathe that we're in America," he said sadly. "I thank God with every beat of my heart for bringing us out."

"I thank God *and* the good Austrian doctor that brought us out in the trunk of his car," Rachel shot back, rattling the coffeepot and clattering cups together. "But I don't dwell on the past like you do."

"Back home she showed me respect," David complained to no one in particular. "Here she gets big ideas."

Grace met Rachel's eyes, and at the same time, they both held up their hands in mock-despair. "It's America, I can get any ideas I want," Rachel insisted.

David grumbled, but he looked at his wife with admiration, nonetheless. Such bickering had become a daily ritual with them, as Rachel became more independent and vivacious in her new life. Still smiling, Grace poured herself a cup of coffee.

"I'm going out to see if my garden has recovered from Mrs. Furness's chickens," she announced.

"Bring in some parsley!" Sarah called after her.

Dew wet the toes of Grace's white tennis shoes as she

stepped into the victory garden behind the house. What had formerly been a formal flower garden had been turned over to vegetables, in aid of the war effort. Yet along the fence, an ancient gnarled rosebush still twined, its red blooms echoing the stripes in the flags that hung in front of every house in town. Grace bent to smell the fragrance of one blossom and then turned back to inspect her rows of vegetables. In a distant yard a dog barked, and someone's screen door shut with a whine. Marblehead was waking up to another fine late summer day. The sky was blue, and the gulls headed out to sea, calling to one another like factory girls going in to the shipyards at the start of a shift.

The back door of the Wild Rose creaked open, and Grace looked around to see Mike come out onto the granite step in his army fatigues and T-shirt. He stretched and scratched his head and yawned. The dog tag around his neck winked in the sunshine.

"You look like you have as much trouble waking up as I do," Grace said with a laugh.

He blinked sleepily. "Good morning. What a day."

Grace sipped her coffee, looking at him over the rim of her cup. Mike projected a sense of calm and stability that made Grace feel instantly at ease. Her sense of happiness in his company surprised her, but it was for Jimmy's sake, she reasoned, that she was glad the two were such friends.

She cupped her coffee cup in both hands. "Mike, can I ask you something?"

"You bet." He sat down on the step and waited calmly for her to speak.

Grace looked down into her coffee. "You're a medic, you treated Jimmy when he got shot. Will you tell me truthfully . . ."

"How bad it was?"

She nodded, and Mike rubbed his chin. "It was pretty bad. I thought at first he'd lose the leg."

"But he's tough," Grace said urgently. "He wouldn't give up without a fight."

"Hmm." Mike pushed himself off the step and began walking along a row of string beans, his head bent and his hands shoved into his pockets. When he reached the end of the row he turned to look back at her. "How does he seem to you?"

Grace had trouble holding his gaze. She looked away, and reached to pull a weed that was sneaking in among the tomatoes. Her mother's caution about war's effects echoed in her ear. "He seems fine, just fine," Grace said in a low voice. "Just the same."

Mike didn't reply, and Grace wondered how she could honestly voice what had first come to her lips—that there was a hard edge to Jimmy that hadn't been there before, that she still hadn't had more than a glimpse of the easygoing, modest boy who had left Marblehead for Europe. She was ashamed of hurrying to judge, however; it was unfair to expect a man in the center of heroic admiration to resist bragging a little bit.

"War's hard," Mike said finally. He picked a string

bean and bit it. "Soldiering makes a guy kind of rough around the edges."

"You don't seem very rough," she said.

"Oh, I hide it well."

Grace was thankful for his kindness and his generosity, and gave him a grateful smile. She only had to give Jimmy time to settle back into the routine of life in Marblehead, she decided, and those rough edges would be rubbed smooth once again. Once the stress and hurry of war was behind him, Jimmy would be fine.

"This place kind of reminds me of where I had my Red Cross training," Mike said, looking up at the back of the inn.

"Really?" Grace asked. "Where was that?"

"In a Quonset hut on Long Island," he replied with a lopsided grin.

Grace cocked her head. "That's not exactly flattering. Our hotel reminds you of an army camp?"

"That's right," Mike replied easily. "Because you couldn't find anything more different—this has got to be the homiest place I've ever been. Swear to God, this is a hell of a house for Jimmy to come home to. He's a lucky guy."

Smiling, Grace stood up and brushed off her knees. "That's the sweetest thing anybody's said to me all day."

"Well, it's still early."

They sat side by side on the old wooden garden bench, and Grace blew over the surface of her coffee while Mike tipped his face to the sunshine. He had the high, wide cheekbones of a Scandinavian. Grace imagined the Vikings looking the way Mike looked, with farseeing eyes and strong hands. She imagined he was good at his job, efficient but kind and gentle to the hurt and wounded.

"Tell me about what you do," Grace said, curious to know more about Jimmy's friend.

Mike shrugged. "First aid, literally. Medics are the first guys to treat the wounded, so it's compression bandages, tourniquets, photos."

"Photos?"

"Betty Grable, Rita Hayworth, any pinup will do for a distraction." Mike gave her a sheepish smile. "I ran out of painkillers a lot."

Grace rose from the bench with a horrified laugh. "I ought to pour my coffee right over your head," she threatened.

"Hey, hold on!" he said, holding up his hands. "I know it sounds lousy, but when you're a medic, you use what works."

Grace tipped the dregs of her coffee onto the ground and shook out the last drops. "You'd think the Army could find a better use for women than just looking pretty for the soldiers. I went to the Red Cross volunteer recruiting office in Boston last year. You know what they said I could do?"

"Search me."

"They said I could be a 'recreation counselor,'" Grace muttered. "That means I'd learn all kinds of vitally useful card games, and would have the honorable duty of distributing cigarettes and toothpaste in army hospitals. I said no thanks."

Mike shook his head. "I guess I don't blame you."

"Well honestly!" Grace exploded. "I'm smart, I'm resourceful. I can make a much greater contribution than that."

"So you work at the fish factory?"

Grace darted a skeptical look his way. "I'm no Rosie the Riveter, but I'm doing my part. And we've been saving paper and scrap metal and grease like crazy, and I've managed to grow all the vegetables we need for the inn. I even take my turn watching the coast for enemy aircraft. I memorized all the silhouettes . . ." She felt a wave of hopelessness rise up in her suddenly, so sharp and bitter that she had to close her eyes. "I thought if I did these things I could bring my dad and my brother and Jimmy and all the other boys home from the war faster."

"Thanks a lot."

She looked up. Mike was smiling at her and Grace felt her cheeks color.

"I really mean it," he went on. "Thank you."

Grace sniffed. "Now *that's* the sweetest thing anybody's said to me all day."

Mike stood up. "And I still say it's still early. Here comes Jimmy. See you later."

Before Grace could protest, Mike took three long strides to the back door. He disappeared inside just as Jimmy came through the garden gate. Grace's heart melted at the very sight of her sweetheart, and she knew she would feel the same elation every time she saw him for all the years to come.

"Good morning," she said, giving him a wide smile.

"Good morning to you." Jimmy planted a kiss on her cheek. "What happened to Mike?"

Grace sighed contentedly. "He had a sudden onset of tact," she explained. "He's giving us some privacy."

"No kidding?" Jimmy glanced at the door and shook his head. "Funny guy."

"You're lucky to have a friend like that," Grace told him.

He turned and took her in his arms, smiling down into her face. "And I'm lucky to have a girl like you. All the time I was hurt I was thinking about you, Grace. Things got pretty crazy sometimes. I thought I was going to die."

Grace put her cheek against his shoulder. "But you didn't die," she whispered. "You don't have to think about it anymore."

"No, let me tell you," he insisted, holding her close and putting his cheek against her hair. "It was thinking about you that pulled me through. If I hadn't known you were here waiting for me—I don't know if I would've made it. Honestly."

"Oh, Jimmy," she breathed.

"My sweet, lovable Grace." He took her hand in his and looked down at it. "Holding your little hand in mine. That's a dream to come home to."

Grace smiled tenderly and put her hand against his

41

cheek. "My hand is bigger now than it was when you left," she said gently.

He brought her fingers to his lips, his eyes dark with emotion. "No, you'll always be my little Grace. Nothing will ever change that."

"Oh, sweetheart," she whispered, a strange catch in her voice. Maybe things really hadn't changed at all.

Chapter Four

GRACE'S FOOTSTEPS RANG on the treads of the iron staircase and echoed off the cinder-block walls. The clang and stamp of canning machines and the odor of fish followed her as she ran up. Voices from the production floor were distorted in the huge, cavernous building, bouncing and reverberating like the calls of undersea animals. Through a gaping door onto the ocean, a load of silver cod poured in from a ship and onto a conveyor belt. Diesel fumes chugged in from the fishing boat's funnels.

"Oh, I wish we had a ladies' room up here!" Grace gasped, ducking into the business office and slamming the door shut behind her. "This entire factory is run by women, but there's just one ladies' room!"

Barbara looked up from her typewriter, her fingers hardly pausing as she rattled away. "Hey, it's an adventure."

With a laugh, Grace sat down at her desk again, and

yanked out the adding machine tape to check where she had left off. From the corner of her eye, she noticed the clock. "Barbie, it's almost four. Let's hear the news."

"Roger." Barbara spun around in her chair and switched on the radio, which was finishing up a musical program.

The girls worked companionably, each competent in her own job, accompanying each other in a steady mechanical percussion that drowned out the sounds of the factory below them. After a moment, Barbara let out a stifled oath and her typewriter fell silent.

"Jammed keys?" Grace knew what it was without looking around. Her fingers tap-tapped on the adding machine, and cranked the handle in a steady rhythm. Behind her, Barbara wrestled with the typewriter.

"How are plans coming for your birthday party?" Barbara asked, slamming the carriage return. The bell "pinged" like a chime.

"It's not a birthday party and you know it," Grace replied. She shuffled some papers, her eyes scanning lists of halibut, cod, and herring, all the bountiful ore of the rich fishing banks. She liked thinking of her father and brother, far away in the Pacific, opening a can of North Atlantic cod and tasting home.

Barbara was humming along with a dance tune. "Well, it's a party, and it's on your birthday," she said in a ruminative tone. "Gosh, I guess I must've been nuts to think it could be a birthday party."

"All right, wise guy," Grace laughed. She added up

more bass, bream, and haddock for her father and brother and the rest of the boys in the Pacific.

"And now, at the top of the hour," came the news announcer's voice.

"Shh-shh," Barbara hissed.

Both girls looked at the radio. Grace pushed both hands against the edge of her desk, as though to ward off bad news.

"From the Pacific Fleet: fighting continues today on the island of Guam, heavy casualties reported in Marine units. Two destroyers, USS *Schuyler* and USS *Columbia,* are lost to mines in the vicinity of Midway."

"God rest all sailors lost at sea," Barbara murmured.

Grace closed her eyes, her heart going out to the families of the men lost, yet deeply, greedily thankful that the ships carried none of her own loved ones. Another day safe.

"Grace."

She turned to see a stricken expression on Barbara's face. "What is it?"

"Mrs. Dugget, Loretta Dugget in Swampscott—she's got a boy on the *Schuyler,*" Barbara whispered, her eyes wide.

A sickening jolt in Grace's stomach made her bow her head in pain. Just last night, gossipy Mrs. Dugget had called to herald Jimmy's return. Now the woman would be hearing the news that her own son would never jump off the Cape Ann bus and wave his hat to her. The star on the service flag in Mrs. Dugget's window would be changed to gold, now. Another Gold Star mother. Another lost son.

"God, sometimes I worry the war will use up all the men," Barbara said. "It's been so long, so many of them are gone . . ." Her own brother was stationed safely in Washington, D.C., and her father was too old for active service. But still, Grace knew Barbara felt the same apprehension that everyone else suffered.

Grace thought of Jimmy and again felt a dizzy rush of relief. For him, the war was over, and she had one less man to wait for. *Now just bring Dad and Mark home,* she prayed silently.

The office door opened. A girl from downstairs, her head tied up in a red bandanna, looked at Grace.

"Messenger for you," she said soberly. "You're needed at home right away."

Grace's heart made another sickening lurch. "Is it my father? My brother? What is it?" she asked, scraping her chair back across the linoleum so fast it crashed over backwards.

"I don't know," the girl apologized. "He didn't say."

The three girls stared silently at one another, all of them fearing the worst. Grace could hear her pulse beating in her ears.

"It could just be your mother wants you," Barbara said in a deliberately calm voice.

"Yes, that could be it," Grace said. She made herself right her chair, and tap the papers on her desk into a neat stack. "If Mr. Tedisco asks about me, tell him I had to— tell him—"

46

"Just go." Barbara put one hand over Grace's. "Go on."

Grace nodded and then hurried out the door. Her heels rattled on the iron staircase, and her fingers slipped on the damp handrail. The smell of raw fish blood and engine oil rising from below made her feel sick. She ran across the wet concrete floor and slammed through the exit into the sunshine.

"At last!"

She whirled around. Jimmy tossed away a cigarette and stepped out of the shadow of the building with a wide, carefree smile on his face. He had found some of his old blue jeans and a white shirt, and looked relaxed and cheerful.

"What is it?" Grace grabbed his arm. "What's happened?"

He raised his eyebrows in a laugh. "Nothing. Don't get so hot under the collar, Grace. I just wanted to see my girl, that's all."

Grace felt the panic rush away from her. Her knees suddenly felt weak. "Oh."

"I just couldn't wait another minute," he added, pulling her into his arms. "How about a kiss?"

"You're crazy," Grace said with a feeble laugh.

"Crazy for you, sure." He kissed her hard on the mouth, and Grace put her hands to his chest and pushed away.

"You really scared me," she told him, trying to look severe but smiling in spite of herself. "Next time, don't give me a heart attack."

She began to walk toward the building, but Jimmy caught her hand. "I do have to get back to work," she explained reluctantly.

He swung her hand back and forth. "No, you don't, it's almost five. I've waited patiently all day, can't we have some time alone before we have dinner with my mother?"

"But Jimmy . . ." Grace didn't know whether to kiss him or pull her hand away. She wished she *could* just jump into the car with him. "I've never played hooky, you know that."

"It's not too late to start," Jimmy told her.

She laughed and threw her arms around his neck. "You've become absolutely wicked, over there among those sophisticated French. Have they been leading you astray?"

"You'll find out," he said, kissing her again.

Grace closed her eyes, savoring his kiss.

Then, behind her, the door opened and Barbara poked her head out. "What is it?" Barbara asked in a tone of concern.

Jimmy's expression soured slightly at Barbara's appearance. "I'll be right back," Grace whispered to him. She ran over to her friend.

"He was just—he just wanted to see me, that's all," Grace explained quietly. She laughed, to show Barbara that it was only a touching prank. But Barbara didn't look particularly touched.

"Don't you know what went through Grace's mind when she heard there was an emergency?" Barbara asked.

Jimmy shrugged and fished a cigarette out of his back pocket. "I'm not a mind reader," he said. "Are you?"

"I didn't have to read her mind," Barbara said dryly. "She thought her father or brother might have been killed."

Grace swallowed hard. Her cheeks felt hot. "Come on, it's over, don't worry about it, Barbie," she pleaded.

"Grace, let's go," Jimmy said, ignoring Barbara. "You can leave a few minutes early. It doesn't matter."

"Cover for me?" Grace asked her friend.

Their eyes met. For a moment, Grace was afraid Barbara was going to make a stink. But a fleeting smile passed over Barbara's face. She shrugged one shoulder and yanked open the door.

"Okay, see you tomorrow."

Grace let her breath out. "Thanks. You're a champ," she said, kissing her friend on the cheek.

She rejoined Jimmy, and he put his arm across her shoulders to lead her to the parking lot. Grace had the uneasy feeling that if she looked back, she'd find Barbara's ironic green eyes on her. Instead, she glanced up at Jimmy, and reminded herself that he had come out of love for her.

"It really was sweet of you," she said.

He grinned, his eyes bright with laughter as he opened the car door for her and handed her in. "We sure took the wind out of her sails."

"She was only worried for me," Grace pointed out.

Jimmy put on an expression of exaggerated surprise.

"*Sacré bleu!* She can mind 'er own beeswax," he said in a phony French accent.

"Jimmy!" Grace shook her head and laughed. "You're impossible."

"Don't you like zat I speak zis way?" he asked her. "Such a useful thing I have learned in ze hospital in France. Among ozzer things," he added, waggling his eyebrows up and down.

Giggling, she leaned over and planted a kiss on his cheek. "You're adorable. And silly."

The tires squealed as he pulled the car out of the factory lot, and he took the oceanside road to the south, the salty wind gusting in through the open windows. Grace took the pins from her hair and shook it loose and leaned back against the seat. Now that the shock of thinking her brother or father might be hurt was wearing off, she could relax. But she still found it almost impossible to believe that Jimmy was really home, that she could be going for a drive with him. Smiling in wonderment, she reached out and caressed his cheek. Without taking his eyes from the road, Jimmy turned to kiss her hand.

"I'm so glad you're back," Grace said, her eyes shining. "Everything is so perfect. Oh, I forgot to tell you something wonderful!"

He switched on the radio and Bing Crosby crooned a love song. "What's the news, honey?"

"Mark wrote that he's going to go to Hollywood when he gets out," Grace said, tucking one foot under her and turning to face Jimmy directly. "He doesn't want to

50

run the Wild Rose. Dad and Mom and I will be partners. And you, too," she added.

"Don't you think I can provide for you?" he asked.

Grace touched his shoulder gently. "Of course I do. But you know running the inn is what I always dreamed of. We used to talk about it all the time. What we would do if you and I ran it, remember?"

"I remember thinking you were adorable, pretending to be a grown-up businesswoman."

"And now I am," Grace said. "I've been running the place with Mom for the past two years now, and I'm so good at it she doesn't mind leaving almost all the decisions to me. And it's been hard, since the war has changed the way all the suppliers operate. And in addition to the day-to-day business, we've had swap meets and scrap drives, and dance marathons to raise money for refugees —anything I can think of to help the war effort. I've had all sorts of ideas."

Jimmy nodded absently, concentrating on the road as she spoke. Beyond his profile, on the cliff's edge, wind-twisted rosebushes swept by in a blur against the glittering ocean.

"That's great, honey."

Grace felt a pang of misgiving. "You used to say you wanted to be there with me," she added hesitantly.

"Oh, sure, Grace. Sure. And I've got ideas, too," he said, giving her a swift smile before looking back at the road. The radio was playing loud, and he had to raise his voice over it. "What I thought was we could turn the rooms into efficiency units with kitchenettes. That way you can charge more and do less cooking, too. We could even turn the dining room into a recreation room. Maybe some pool tables or something."

Grace frowned and turned down the radio. "But people like eating in the dining room," she pointed out.

"It's so old-fashioned," Jimmy scoffed. "Trust me, I've done a lot of traveling in the last couple years. England, France, and I've seen a lot of hotels. I say forget serving meals altogether. Concentrate on one thing."

"We do concentrate on one thing." Grace tried to keep her disappointment from sounding in her voice. "Being an inn. That means rooms and meals."

Jimmy laughed and turned the radio back up. The Glenn Miller Band was blasting out a swing tune. "We'll see."

Grace tried to imagine the dining room of the Wild Rose turned into a pool hall. "I don't think that—"

"What?" he raised his voice over the big band music.

"Nothing." A surge of anger, so strong and sudden that it shocked her, rose in Grace. She flexed her hands, which were tense from working the adding machine all afternoon. "Let's get to your house. Your mother will wonder where we are."

He smiled at her, his old Jimmy smile. "You're right. She's pulling out all the stops for dinner tonight. My mom is the best cook in the world, too, you know."

The look in his eyes flooded Grace with relief. Here was the sweet Jimmy she had been waiting for. She shook herself mentally. It was only that she'd been so spoiled by making all important decisions on her own that she found

52

it difficult to make allowances and compromises, she reasoned. She had always wanted and expected Jimmy to work at the Wild Rose with her, and it was only fair in a partnership to listen to new ideas.

" 'Do I love you, do I? Doesn't one and one make two?' " he sang with the radio.

" 'Do I love you, do I? Does July need a sky of blue?' " Grace continued, her doubts blowing out the window on the breeze. She was in love with him. She was sure she was.

He sent her a wink, and Grace knew she was an idiot to worry. She scooted closer to him on the seat, and for the rest of the drive to his mother's house, kept her hand tucked into his arm and her head on his shoulder. As they turned the corner, they passed Mr. Staines's scrap-metal truck, which clanked and clanged with a ragtag jumble of iron. Jimmy tooted the horn and waved, and Mr. Staines gave them a jaunty wave in return.

"How can there be a single piece of metal left in this town to melt down?" Jimmy asked, laughing as he parked at the curb. "They'll be asking for the pipes out of our houses, next."

"They can have the roof over my head, as long as they don't ask for you to go back to the war," Grace told him with a loving smile.

He grinned and ushered her ahead of him into his house.

"Oh, here you are!" Mrs. Penworthy cried the moment they stepped inside. "Come in, come in."

"I've been gone two hours, Mom. Did you really miss

53

me that much?" Jimmy asked as he kissed his widowed mother's cheek. His limp seemed much more pronounced as he walked in.

"Of course I missed you," Mrs. Penworthy said. Taking both of Grace's hands, Jimmy's mother looked at her tearfully. "You make the sweetest couple, I always said."

"Knock it off, Mom," Jimmy laughed. He passed by his mother and went into the living room and seated himself in a worn leather wing chair. "And don't worry, I didn't use up all the gas. I've got plenty of ration stamps, anyway."

"Oh, what do I care?" his mother said, bustling in after him and pushing a footstool within his reach. "I haven't minded not driving, but you—with your leg? You deserve to drive."

Jimmy grinned at Grace over his mother's head and then sat back with a sigh of contentment. "My buddy Mike hasn't shown yet, huh?"

"Not yet, sweetheart, but I'm sure he'll be here soon. Now let me get you some nice cold lemonade. I just made it."

"Thanks, Mom." Jimmy stretched his legs out and sighed with contentment.

Grace, with a wryly amused glance at Jimmy, strolled into the living room and sat on the arm of the couch. "Your mother sure dotes on you," she said with a chuckle.

"Sure, why not?" Jimmy asked as the doorbell rang. "Could you get that, Grace? I bet it's Mike. I'd get up, but my leg—"

"Of course, sweetheart," Grace said, mimicking, her

eyes twinkling. She went to the door, marveling to herself that she had never noticed before just how much Mrs. Penworthy fawned over her only son. She was smiling as she opened the door.

Mike stood there. He blinked in surprise when he saw Grace. "Wow."

"Wow what?" she asked, smiling even wider.

"You look—so pretty," he replied, somewhat falteringly.

"You're just saying that because you haven't seen girls in so long," Grace said with a laugh. She hooked her arm through his, feeling happy and lighthearted to have him there. "Come on into the castle. King Jimmy awaits your presence."

"Hey, Mike, how are ya?" Jimmy greeted Mike without rising from his chair, and Mrs. Penworthy bustled back in, wiping her hands on her frilled apron.

"It's such a pleasure to have you here, Mike. Come on into the dining room, everyone. Dinner's ready. I made all your favorites," she added to Jimmy.

Jimmy winked at Mike. "Mothers. You know how they are."

Mike didn't say anything. He just grinned and waved Grace ahead of him in to dinner.

"I'm sure you boys didn't get a decent meal the whole time you were away," Mrs. Penworthy said as they all seated themselves.

"If I never eat another baked bean in my life, I'll be satisfied," Mike agreed.

"And I was planning to serve nothing but baked beans at my party," Grace said with a sigh.

Mike grinned, and Jimmy, helping himself to carrots, looked over at Grace. "What party?"

"Her birthday party, dear," Mrs. Penworthy put in quickly.

"It's not a birthday party," Grace insisted. "It's another dance at the Wild Rose, and it happens to be on my birthday. That's all. No special occasion."

Mrs. Penworthy heaped more carrots on Jimmy's plate, and moved the salt and pepper within his reach. "Maybe we can expect some kind of announcement at the party?" she asked with an arch smile. "Make a proper celebration of it?"

Grace met Jimmy's eyes. He winked. "Just you wait, Mom."

Grace blushed and her gaze happened to fall on Mike. He met her eyes and smiled, and she blushed even deeper.

"Mom, isn't there any butter?" Jimmy asked.

"We can't get butter, dear, it's oleomargarine. I'll get it," his mother said.

"No, let me," Grace broke in quickly, feeling suddenly very strange and nervous. She pushed herself away from the table and hurried into the kitchen. She didn't know what had her so shook up, but she was suddenly as rattled as if someone had asked her to give a piano recital, bake a three-tier cake, dance a foxtrot, and darn some socks all at the same time.

Drawing a deep breath, she looked at the kitchen

table with its red-checked oilcloth and the sugar bowl shaped like a frog. Years ago, she had sat there, watching adoringly as Jimmy showed her how to do long division.

"It's a piece of cake, Gracie," he had said. "See if you can do it, and I'll give you a surprise if you get it right."

He had seemed perfect and wonderful to her, back then. She had felt a hero worship for him that made him larger than life, wiser and kinder than anyone else, able to do anything at all. But now that he was an authentic hero, she couldn't remember what that worship felt like, and she couldn't help but wonder if Jimmy would expect her to wait on him the way his mother did.

On the floor by the back door was a can of grease from cooking, and a neatly tied bundle of paper for the next collection. Even Mrs. Penworthy, all alone in the house, was doing her share to supply the war factories with the raw materials that everyone contributed. Had Jimmy thanked her, Grace wondered. Did he recognize the effort his mother had made to keep the Army running? So far, he hadn't recognized Grace's efforts, and she admitted to herself that it stung.

"Grace?" Jimmy's voice reached her from the dining room.

"I'll be right there," she called, yanking open the refrigerator. She picked up a milk bottle and held the cold glass to her cheek for a moment. Then she put it back and reached for the margarine.

"How were the fish today?" Mike asked as she returned to the table.

"Smelly as ever." Grace set the margarine down, and

resumed her seat without looking at Jimmy. "You might think you'd get used to it, but—"

"Say, Grace," Jimmy interrupted. "If you're having a party, you'll probably need to get more ration stamps."

Grace was embarrassed by his rudeness, but she smiled it away. "I know. I trade for them. I've been doing it for years."

"Because people expect a party to be something special, a break from ordinary routine," he continued, spreading margarine on a hot roll. He pointed the knife at her for emphasis. "They'll want to feel like they don't need to scrimp and save."

"I know, Jimmy," Grace said again. Across the table, she could see that Mike looked embarrassed by Jimmy's manner, too. "Don't worry about the party. I have everything under control."

"She does, too," Mrs. Penworthy said eagerly. Her round, anxious face was flushed with pride. "You should see her, Jimmy. She's such a good little businesswoman."

Jimmy pulled his mouth into a wry smile. "Sure, Mom. She's a regular Howard Hughes."

There was an uncomfortable silence. Through the open window, the sound of a car went puttering by.

"So how long have the Teitelbaums lived with you?" Mike asked Grace, changing the subject.

"Two years," she replied with relief. "Little Nathan is so adorable, and he's learned English so quickly."

"I bet you taught him," Mike said.

Grace gave a self-deprecating wave of her hand. "I might have helped a little."

"How long do they think they're staying?" Jimmy asked, reaching for the rolls again. "They can't sponge off the Wild Rose forever."

"They can stay as long as they want," Grace replied firmly. She found she couldn't look at him. "And they're not sponging, they work very hard."

Jimmy shrugged. "Well, once the GIs are demobilized, you should give the jobs to Americans. After all, the Teitelbaums are Germans."

"They're Jewish refugees," Grace said, frowning down at her plate. She pushed her carrots aside with her fork. "And they'll become American citizens soon enough, Jimmy." Her voice quavered slightly.

"Hey, okay, okay," he said. "I guess they're staying." He smiled tenderly. "You sure are their champion."

"Jim, remember that time we went to London for the weekend?" Mike poured himself a glass of milk, never taking his eyes off Jimmy. "What was the name of that funny little pub where we danced on the tables?"

"Danced on the tables?" Mrs. Penworthy looked delightfully scandalized. "You boys must have gotten into all kinds of trouble."

"Well, that was just the beginning," Mike said, and for the next twenty minutes, regaled them with tales of their hijinks with Vic. "The terrible trio, they called us," he said.

"And don't forget that old guy on the steps of the British Museum," Jimmy said with a laugh.

Mike nodded. "That's right. We went to see the Elgin Marbles. And this crazy old coot . . ."

Grace let her mind drift as Mike and Jimmy reminisced, and only pulled herself out of her reverie when she noticed the time.

"Oh, I've got to go," she announced, rising from the table. "Mrs. Penworthy, that was a wonderful dinner. I'm so sorry I can't stay to help clean up."

"Don't you worry about a thing, dear."

Looking crestfallen, Jimmy gazed up at her and shook his head. "Why do you have to go? I thought we could watch some of those old home movies."

"But it's my turn to take an hour watching for enemy aircraft from the cliffs," Grace apologized. "I can't stay."

Jimmy made as though to stand up. "Well, at least I can walk with—"

His mother let out a horrified gasp. "Jimmy, your leg! You're not marching around on the cliffs if I have anything to say about it."

"Oh, all right," he agreed, settling back in. He sent Grace an apologetic smile. "I hate to let you go all alone."

"I'll go with you, Grace," Mike offered. "I'd like to get some exercise."

Grace threw up her hands in exasperation. "Honest to Pete! I've been doing this on my own for months." The others looked startled by her vehemence, and Grace laughed sheepishly. "But I'd be happy for some company, Mike. Then I can get all the really juicy gossip about London and Paris."

"Tell her how a farm boy from Minnesota gets along in a posh nightclub," Jimmy suggested, his eyes full of mischief.

60

Mike was unfazed. "Maybe I'll tell her how you got so drunk you danced with the performing bear—"

"It's a lie!" Jimmy blustered, laughing. "An outrageous fabrication."

Giggling, Grace led the way to the door. "Let me just pick up my binoculars at home, and we're on our way."

Twenty minutes later, they had made the walk to the cliffs and were seated on a granite boulder overlooking the wide sweep of the Atlantic. The sky was streaked in purple and orange, and the white sails of pleasure boats coming in for the night reflected the sunset colors like live coals. Grace raised the heavy binoculars to her eyes and scanned the eastern horizon.

"I love such a wide open view, don't you?" Grace asked.

Mike sat back against the sun-warmed rock. "It reminds me of home."

"Home, is that Minnesota, like Jimmy said?"

"Mmhmm. Western Minnesota, out on the prairie. You can see for miles and miles, just like this," Mike replied. "It's an ocean of grass, wheat, and corn."

Grace made another sweep of the sky with her binoculars and then put them down in her lap. "Will you have time to visit your family while you're on leave?"

Mike squinted at the horizon, his blue eyes focused far away. "I don't have any family. I was orphaned twice. Once as a baby, and then in high school. The old folks who adopted me died," he explained.

"I'm so sorry." Grace picked up the binoculars again, wishing she hadn't asked.

61

"Don't be," Mike told her easily. "In the Army, I feel like I've got a huge family. I like it."

"Is Jimmy a brother to you?" Grace asked in a low voice.

While she waited for his answer, the wind swept her hair back from her temples. She remembered what Jimmy had said to Mike about mothers: You know how mothers are. But Jimmy must have known Mike was orphaned. Grace frowned to think that Jimmy would be so insensitive. As she scowled into the binoculars, she realized Mike hadn't answered her. Finally, she had to lower the glasses again.

"Is he a brother to you?"

Mike met her eyes with a nod. "He's a brother to me," Mike agreed. "I'd do anything for him. Anything."

A wave of compassion and shame caught Grace and made her shiver. She knew she should make more allowances for Jimmy, feel as Mike did, that she'd do anything for him. Mike's plain loyalty filled her with admiration. Grace had a strong desire to take his hand, but, startled by her own impulse, she gripped the binoculars even tighter.

"I'm glad you came back with him," she said.

He looked at her, and then away. "Me too."

Grace fidgeted with the binoculars, adjusting the leather strap. "How long can you stay?"

"My tour is up when my leave is over," he said in a thoughtful, considering voice. "I'm thinking about taking another assignment in France. Or even the Pacific theater. They need medics out there in the worst way."

An image came to Grace of a man lying facedown on a beach, palm trees rustling in the wind as the surf washed over the dead soldier's feet. She shuddered.

"Cold?" Mike asked.

"My father and my brother are out there," she whispered.

Mike stood up and was silhouetted against the darkening sky. Grace felt another shudder pass through her. The war wasn't over. Not yet. There were still plenty of men to be killed, and plenty of grief ahead.

"Don't go," she said impulsively.

He reached a hand to help her up. "We'll see," he said in a faraway tone. "I haven't decided yet. They'll let me go to medical school now if I want, but they need me."

Their hands were still clasped together. In the cool breeze, his fingers were warm around hers. Without a word, she withdrew her hand, and they stood together, watching the lights of a freighter on the Atlantic.

Grace wrapped her arms around herself tightly. "A ship taking supplies to Europe. Whenever I see one, I always say a prayer that it'll come back to port safe," she said, but her eyes were on Mike, and not on the ship at sea.

Chapter Five

GRACE SAID GOOD NIGHT to Mike outside the Wild Rose and watched him go into the tavern. She slipped around the side of the house in the darkness and let herself in through the back door. The kitchen was empty but the radio was on, and its voice in the room made the kitchen feel even emptier. Grace stood in the doorway, her head bowed.

"Ah, here you are," Mrs. MacKenzie said, coming in through the opposite door.

"Where is everyone?" Grace asked.

"David's out front, and Rachel is putting Nathan to bed," her mother said. She opened the refrigerator. "How about a slice of pie? I'm getting one for Mr. Potter."

Grace shook her head but sat at the kitchen table. There were several pairs of green Bakelite salt and pepper shakers from the dining room there, waiting to be refilled. She toyed with them, pouring a few grains of salt onto the table and trying to balance a shaker on the crystals. She concentrated on her task, her brow creased. A sense of incompleteness clung to her. The shaker toppled over.

"How was dinner?" Her mother cut a piece of cherry pie and slid it deftly onto a glass plate. "Did you have a good time with Jimmy?"

A lump came to Grace's throat. "I guess so," she said quietly, trying again to balance the salt shaker on the table. Her hand shook, knocking the salt shaker over again.

Her mother sat down and placed one hand over Grace's. "Did something happen? You look miserable."

"No, it's only . . ." Grace turned her head, listening to the soft voice on the radio in an ad for US War Bonds. "Jimmy seems so changed."

Her mother was silent. Grace looked at her, the color flaming into her cheeks. "I know what I said this morning. But tonight I couldn't help noticing that he's—"

"Not the same boy at all?" Mrs. MacKenzie finished for her. She stroked Grace's hand and nodded.

"He never used to be so bossy, so—so prickly." Grace struggled with her thoughts. "Remember years ago when he taught Mark how to tie sailing knots?"

Mrs. MacKenzie laughed, her dark eyes warm with the memory. "Poor Mark was so clumsy. He still is."

"But Jimmy was so patient and relaxed," Grace said. Her voice tightened. "I know he's only been back for one day, but I keep wondering when he's going to be himself again. I've seen glimpses of the old Jimmy, but just glimpses. And mostly he treats me like a little girl, and I get the feeling that he's looking at me, but not really seeing me. He's seeing the little girl I used to be."

"Well, that's the picture he's carried with him since he left."

Slowly, Grace shook her head. She felt tired and dispirited. "He used to be able to see everything so clearly."

Her mother listened for a moment to the radio. The news was on, and the announcer was giving a report of fighting in France. "War," Hope said. "God, it can hurt soldiers in so many ways. And us. Every day I wonder if it's going to kill me."

"But the fighting will never come here," Grace said in alarm.

Mrs. MacKenzie's dark eyes filled with tears. "I don't expect to be shot, sweetheart. But waiting from day to day, wondering if Bob or Mark will be killed, knowing that there's *nothing* I can do to prevent it—it's harder than anything, even fighting, I think. All I can do is write and write, trying to make it hurt less."

"They'll come home, just like Jimmy did." Grace swallowed hard. "I know they will. You'll see."

"If they don't, I won't want to live."

Grace's heart lurched painfully. "You don't mean that."

Her mother nodded. She wasn't melodramatic or sentimental, only truthful. "If either of my men dies, it will kill me."

Silence fell between them, and the radio report filled it with casualties, anti-tank fire, bridges mined, French collaborators arrested. Grace heard the hateful, wounding words and felt them drop on her heart like poison. Her mother's vehemence filled her with shame.

"I don't know if I ever felt that way about Jimmy," she whispered. The radio continued its list of horrors, the beautiful names of French villages made ugly by war.

"Mom, don't I love him?"

Standing abruptly, Mrs. MacKenzie strode across the kitchen and yanked the radio plug from the wall. "I can't answer that for you."

Grace covered her eyes with one hand, seeing the lamplight red between her fingers. *Can I answer it?* she asked herself. *Can I?*

She sat cloaked in her doubts, questioning her heart, as her mother arranged the pie and a napkin and fork on a tray. Then she glanced at the clock on the wall. It was just shy of nine.

"How many people do we have out front?" she asked.

Mrs. MacKenzie shrugged and picked up the tray. "Not more than usual. Why? Are you going out again?"

"If you think you can get along without me," Grace said.

"I expect we can manage," her mother replied with a tiny smile. "Go on."

Grace paused to give her mother a kiss on the cheek and then hurried out the door again. The evening streets were hushed and scented with nighttime blooms: hot sweet carnations and flowering tobacco. She turned onto the Penworthys' street. A quick glance told her that the household was still awake. Light burned in the downstairs windows. She ran lightly up the front steps and rapped on the door and then counted to twelve before Jimmy opened the door, throwing an oblong of light over her.

"How about we watch those movies now?" Grace asked, smiling.

Jimmy grinned from ear to ear. "Hey, that's a swell idea. Come on in."

Limping, he preceded her through the hall into the living room. Mrs. Penworthy looked up from knitting a khaki green watch cap.

"Why, Grace, you came back."

Grace nodded. She was filled with remorse for judging her sweetheart so harshly, and without thinking, she reached for his hand.

"It's all ready to go," Jimmy said eagerly, moving to a table where the projector was set up. Hobart Penworthy, Jimmy's father, had been rich and self-indulgent, and had bought every newfangled gadget that came along. So even in the late thirties, he had had a hand-held movie camera, still a novelty in most circles. Grace pulled the blackout shades and settled herself on the sofa, watching as Jimmy threaded the first reel.

"I don't even know what's on these," he said in a happy voice. "We never labeled them."

In a moment, he had the projector running, the lights switched off, and had seated himself beside Grace. She snuggled against him as he put his arm around her shoulder. The projector hummed and clicked as the film leader flashed bright.

From blackness, Jimmy's own face suddenly shone on the wall, smiling and carefree and handsome.

"You look so young!" Grace exclaimed.

"I think Mark shot this," Jimmy said.

Grace nodded. He had let her brother use the camera whenever he wanted to, since even as a child, Mark saw himself as a film director. Whenever he could get out of his chores at the Wild Rose, Mark had begged or borrowed the movie camera, and had shot reels and reels of Jimmy and Grace.

In the dark, the smoke from Jimmy's cigarette wreathed through the projection. Grace smiled nostalgically to see a younger Jimmy standing on the end of Marblehead Neck at the base of the lighthouse. It was a brilliant day, and he was squinting into the camera. Then into the frame skipped Grace herself, skinny and awkward and pigtailed in a gingham shirt and cutoff shorts. Jimmy's mouth moved as he spoke to her, and she laughed, an expression of wide-eyed adoration on her face. Then they both knelt down on the short, springy grass, and turned headstands.

"Head over heels in love," Jimmy said over the projector's steady hum.

Grace nodded, a lump in her throat. There was no mistaking the two of them in the silent film, and she could even remember that day clearly. But it was still hard to believe it was them. In the movie, Jimmy kicked his legs down and stood upright, and then grabbed Grace's ankles to "wheelbarrow" her around the grass. Grace could see her younger self giggling helplessly under the blue sky, and Jimmy mugging for the camera. He was the Jimmy of all her most treasured memories, smiling constantly, fun-loving, and full of affection for everyone. As the camera moved in closer on Jimmy, he held up his arms in a muscle-man pose, and then threw his head back and laughed, his teeth gleaming in his tanned face.

Then the film went glaring white and ran out of the projector, flap-flapping with a busy racket as it rolled onto the reel.

"Hmm," Jimmy said. "That didn't last very long, did it?"

"No," Grace replied in an absent voice. "No. It didn't last as long as I expected, either."

The next day, it was arranged that Grace, Jimmy, Mike, and Barbara would double date at the new miniature golf course in the evening. It had been Jimmy's suggestion, and he had won out over Grace's protest that he shouldn't do too much walking while he was still recovering from his leg injury. But Jimmy had been stubbornly insistent.

"I thought you'd be happy to go, Grace," he had complained over the telephone. "A guy gets home from the Army, from a pretty rough time fighting and all. He likes to have a little fun."

Grace fidgeted with the papers beside her adding machine. The noise of the factory was giving her a headache. "But we could go to the movies," Grace replied. "Don't you want to see the new Betty Grable picture?"

But he dug his heels in. "You don't have to baby me. I don't expect special treatment."

Hanging up the phone, Grace told herself irritably that that was precisely what he was expecting. But she tried to put that notion out of her head and tell herself that at last they were just going to relax and have fun: no mothers to please, no neighbors to visit, just a night on the town with good friends. Finally, they would have a chance to recapture the easy, unforced magic they had once shared.

"Jimmy and Mike will pick us up here after work," Grace said to Barbara. "And we'll get fried clams or something."

Her friend interleaved carbon paper with some foolscap and rolled it into the typewriter. "Fine. That sounds swell."

Grace darted a suspicious look at Barbara. "Don't you want to go?"

"Oh, sure," Barbara said with a smile.

"You do like Mike, don't you?"

"He seems like a really terrific guy, sure." With another sunny smile, Barbara began to type at a fast clip, the noise making more talk impossible.

Grace leaned over and put her hand on the carriage of the typewriter. Barbara stopped, fingers poised over the keys. She didn't look up.

"You don't like Jimmy, is that it?" Grace asked. She tried to sound breezy. "Because I know for a fact you like fried clams."

With a sigh, Barbara dropped her hands to her lap

and met Grace's eyes. "Look. It doesn't matter if I like Jimmy or not. All that matters is that you do."

"Hmm."

"Don't you 'hmm' me," Barbara said brusquely. "Now hurry up and finish your work so we'll be ready when the guys get here."

Grace said nothing more about it, but she felt an uncomfortable certainty that Barbara and Jimmy would not get along that evening—or any evening. And two hours later, when the four of them arrived at the miniature golf course, she was even more convinced.

"I'll help you with your stroke, Grace," Jimmy offered as they walked arm-in-arm to rent clubs.

"Gosh," Barbara spoke up. She batted her eyelashes at Mike. "And will you help me with mine, Mike?"

He laughed. "I don't think you need any help, Barbara."

"And neither does Grace." Barbara gave Jimmy a wide-eyed, innocent look. "But you know that already, right? You've known Grace all her life."

Jimmy frowned, fishing in his pocket for money. "That's right. I have."

"Hardly seems that way," Barbara muttered.

"I know her better than you do."

Grace held up both hands. "Knock it off, you two. And remember, these clubs are for hitting balls with, not each other."

Jimmy shrugged. "I don't know what's eating her. I don't have a beef with Barbara. She's the one doing all the griping."

Barbara looked at Grace, her eyes stormy, and she gave Jimmy an exaggerated smile. "What a relief. Here I thought you objected to my personality."

Mike held his golf club by the head and swung it between two fingers. He met Grace's eyes with a mischievous grin. "I think we should make them partners. What do you say?"

"Good idea," Grace said. She hooked her arm through Mike's and stuck her tongue out at Jimmy. "And we're going to beat the pants off you."

Before Jimmy or Barbara could object, Grace and Mike strolled off to the first hole. "Serves them right," Grace said, giggling. "I'm tired of their snapping."

"They're just jealous of each other," Mike said. He glanced back over his shoulder to watch Jimmy and Barbara squabble over who would keep score. Mike laughed. "And who can blame them for wanting more of your attention?"

Grace gave him a self-mocking smile. "I can. I can think of a lot more interesting things to fight over than me."

"I can't," Mike said.

Startled, Grace laughed and shook her head. "What a poverty of the imagination," she teased. "I'm going to have a good time in spite of them, and I'm going to have fun with you, since they're more interested in bickering. Come on, let's see if we can beat them to the windmill."

The evening was balmy and fine, and jaunty swing tunes hummed from speakers up on utility poles. Pennants snapped in the breeze, and the excited giggles of small children floated on the breeze. In no time, the four of them were caught up in the competition, although Grace couldn't help noticing that Jimmy took it all more seriously than anyone else.

"I should have made that shot," he grumbled as his ball mysteriously missed the opening of a railroad tunnel.

Mike lined up his next shot and putted carefully. Barbara sneezed loudly just as he hit the ball.

"Oh, too bad," Barbara laughed. Mike's ball rolled into a miniature sand trap with a plywood palm tree planted in it. "Lousy shot."

Mike slapped one hand to his forehead. "Now I'm sunk. The desert island. Come on, Grace. See if you can get stranded with me."

"Forget it." Grace executed a perfect putt.

"You're a dead duck, Holmquist," Jimmy said when it was his turn. "You'll never make it out of there alive."

Grace tugged Mike's sleeve. He bent down so she could whisper in his ear. "Can we use croquet rules? We could bump Jimmy and Barbara right off course."

"It's up to you, partner," he whispered back. Loudly, he added, "I only went into the sand trap as a diversionary tactic. To lure you into a dream of false security."

Barbara snorted. "I doubt that. I think you're just a lousy player."

Giggling, Grace marked her score. She thought Mike was wonderful company, and furthermore, they made a good team: they were winning. The ocean breeze tossed her hair back from her forehead and pressed her skirt against her legs. Jimmy came up behind her as Barbara and Mike continued bantering, and looked over her shoulder.

"You and Mike seem to have a lot of secrets together," he said in an offhand tone.

She laughed and brushed the hair from her forehead. "Are you jealous?"

"Should I be?" he asked, and then added smoothly, "Just kidding. I know I can trust you. Are you sure you added that right?" he asked as he glanced down at Grace's scorecard.

"Positive," she replied, holding the card against her chest. "And don't be silly about Mike. Besides," she added, when Barbara let out a hoot of laughter, "it looks like he and Barbara are really hitting it off."

Jimmy limped a pace away, using the golf club as a cane. He frowned across the course at Barbara and Mike. "She reminds me of your mother. Full of opinions."

"What do you mean, 'full of opinions'? Isn't that a good thing?" Grace asked.

"I guess it depends on what's behind the opinions," he said with a shrug. He sighted along his club, lining up his next shot to the wishing well. "Barbara, your mom. You know."

Grace drew her eyebrows together. "Could you explain yourself?"

"I just mean that people have to have respect for the person in order to respect the opinions."

With growing indignation, Grace took Jimmy's arm and made him face her. "I know you don't like Barbara much, but exactly what are you suggesting about my mother? Are you saying people don't respect her?"

Jimmy smiled uncertainly. "Well, Grace. After all, it's a pretty well-known fact that she was—you know, expecting—when your folks got married."

Hot color washed across Grace's cheeks. The wind tugged a lock of hair across her eyes and she brushed it aside impatiently. "It's a well-known fact because my parents have never made a secret of it. My mother has never tried to hide anything from anybody. She's entirely honest. I think that deserves respect."

She faced him down, waiting for him to apologize. From the corner of her eye, she saw Mike and Barbara look their way, and then walk out of earshot. Gradually, Jimmy broke away from her steely gaze and laughed uncomfortably. "Well, sure, I didn't mean anything by it, Grace. Boy, I guess you gals all have pretty strong opinions these days. I'll have to watch my step," he joked.

She stared at the ground, angry and hurt and bewildered. Ahead, by the little covered bridge, Barbara laughed uproariously at something that Mike said. Grace was suddenly filled with loneliness and frustration, and she longed to know what Mike had said that was so funny.

With a frown, she shoved her club into Jimmy's hand. "I have to go to the ladies' room," she said in a loud voice.

Barbara looked over and handed her club to Mike. "I'll go with you."

They walked in silence across the course, making

their way to the "clubhouse." Two girls in pigtails ran across their path, singing "Soldier Boy." Inside the ladies' room, a buxom blond woman was checking her lipstick in the mirror, and Grace took her hairbrush out of her purse and began fussing with her hair.

"Mike is a riot," Barbara said, taking out a compact and powdering her nose.

A tiny frown creased Grace's forehead. "Do you like him?" she asked casually.

"Oh, sure." Barbara opened her eyes wide and brushed a fleck of mascara off her lashes. "He's not my type, though. Too corn-fed and gentlemanly. I think I go for the tough Robert Mitchum type."

Grace continued brushing her hair carefully, her eyes on her own reflection. She was oddly pleased by Barbara's answer. But realizing how pleased she was gave her a twinge of uneasiness. Grace wanted Mike to stick around.

And she wasn't at all sure what to make of that.

Chapter Six

Two days later, Grace sat going over plans for the party with Rachel after lunch. "I've got plenty of sugar stamps," Grace said, pouring coffee for both of them. She sat down again at the kitchen table. "I know as long as we have enough eggs, sugar, and flour, Sarah can whip up a fantastic cake.

"The birthday cake," Rachel said.

Grace wagged one finger. "Uh-uhn. It's not a birthday party, remember?"

"Maybe a betrothal party, then?" Rachel asked with a coaxing smile.

"In America we call that an engagement party," Grace replied, sidestepping the question. She looked over her list of things to get ready and tried to find an excuse to leave the room before the conversation went further. "There's a wonderful silver punch bowl up in the attic. I think it's hidden away in some box, somewhere. I'll go scavenging."

"Did someone say scavenge?" Mike walked in through the back door, a damp towel around his shoulders and unlaced tennis shoes flopping on his feet. "I'm pretty good at that. Need some help?"

"I need something from the attic," Grace said. "And it might require shoving and wrestling some boxes around. Are you game?"

He saluted. "Yes, ma'am. At your service."

Smiling, she led the way out of the kitchen, down a long corridor along the axis of the hotel. She glanced at his swimming trunks and tennis shoes. "Had a good swim?"

"Great. I love the ocean. Back home, we swam in cowponds. It's not quite the same thrill," he said with a chuckle. "For one thing, we don't get very big waves, except when all the heifers come charging in at the same time."

Grace laughed with him. "I love the ocean, too. It makes me feel like I can do anything."

"I think I know exactly what you mean." They stopped in front of a narrow door. "Is this it?"

"Yes."

She watched him as he opened the door to a back staircase leading to a storeroom. He had a reassuring ability to understand her: it made her believe she could tell him anything. She climbed up the dim stairs, hearing his footsteps behind her, and wondered if she could confide in him her doubts over Jimmy. If anyone could understand and help her sort through her feelings, she was sure

79

Mike could. Considering his own history with Jimmy, he was probably the only person who could.

But something held her back. She paused at the top of the stairs, feeling along the wall for the light switch. Nothing happened when she flicked it up. The only light came from two windows, where two shafts of sunlight fell through the dust motes floating in their path.

"Your eyes will adjust," Mike said matter-of-factly. "We'll be able to see."

They ambled among boxes and furniture, their steps echoing in the quiet attic. Mike ran one finger over the top of a brassbound sea chest. "Lots of junk up here."

"There would have been even more," Grace said as she squeezed between two old iron bedsteads. "But there was a fire here in 1898." She peered into the dimness.

"What are we looking for, anyway?"

"A crate marked 'Logan,' " she said. She sneezed.

Mike wandered away, shoving aside boxes and glancing at their labels. In front of one of the windows, he stopped. "Is this it? It says 'Claire Logan.' "

"Yes."

Grace and Mike knelt before the knee-high crate and together pushed back the lid. It was filled with straw, and Grace dug her hand in, giving Mike an anxious look.

"I hope there aren't any mice in here."

He grinned and plunged his hands in, too. Grace jumped slightly as their fingers touched in the straw and then she dug down deeper and grasped cold metal. She let out a gasp of relief. "Here it is."

She drew out an elegant silver punch bowl and held

it up to the window, turning it to catch the light that gleamed along its side.

"This was a wedding present for my Aunt Claire," Grace said. "She and her husband, Hank, met here during Prohibition and managed to put a gang of bootleggers in jail. Now they run a newspaper in Key West, and they say silver tarnishes too easily down there. I can't imagine putting away a wedding present . . ."

"Why not?" Mike touched the silver bowl and took it from her to examine the engraving. His handsome face was lit from the side, throwing a shadow from his eyelashes onto his high cheekbone. Grace turned her gaze back to the bowl.

"Presents are only someone else's symbol of a marriage," he said quietly. "But as long as the couple love each other and are together, why do they need things like this? Silver tarnishes, but love doesn't."

His voice was low and grave. Grace raised her eyes to his face, and he met her gaze with a warm smile. They looked at one another for a long moment, until Grace broke away.

"I don't know if love tarnishes or not," she murmured.

Mike didn't answer. She knew he was looking at her.

"I'll take that, thanks," she said, reaching for the bowl he still held. Their hands met, and between them the bowl filled up with sunlight, dazzling Grace. She felt her pulse race. Neither of them pulled their hands away until Mike cleared his throat.

"Sorry." He let go of the bowl and Grace rose awkwardly to her feet. She couldn't look up at Mike, but stood gazing blankly out the window. Something had just happened between them, but she wasn't at all sure what. She looked into the silver punch bowl, as if she hoped to find the answer there. Mike moved away, almost stumbling in his haste to put distance between them.

"Hey!" Jimmy's voice floated up the staircase. "Are you two going to make me climb these stairs?"

The color blazed across Grace's cheeks. "We're just getting something!" she called, clutching the bowl to her chest. "We're coming right down."

With clumsy haste Grace pushed her way among the boxes and old furniture to the head of the stairs. She heard Mike following her.

Jimmy was standing at the bottom, peering up into the attic with a petulant frown. He held a cane in one hand. "What are you guys doing up there?"

"Nothing!" Grace spoke vehemently and began a rapid descent. She brushed past Jimmy, who stepped aside.

"Hey, Jim. What have you been up to?" Mike asked as he came down.

Jimmy was still scowling as he eyed Mike's bathing suit. "Not swimming, I can tell you that."

"Is your leg hurting you?" Grace asked nervously.

"Yes, but I'll be fine," he snapped. He moved down the hall, leaning hard on the cane.

Grace met Mike's eyes. Mike hurried to catch up with Jimmy.

"How about I take a look at your leg?" he asked.

"No!" Jimmy held up his cane in defense. "I don't need your interfering."

Mike stopped as though he'd been struck. "All right." He looked at Grace. "I guess I'll go change."

Without another word, Mike headed for the lobby and the main stairs. Grace held the silver bowl so hard her knuckles turned white.

"Coming?" Jimmy asked. "I thought we'd go for a drive."

She stared at him, shaking her head in disbelief. "You didn't have to talk to Mike that way. He's only trying to help you."

"Why are you sticking up for him?"

"Because you're behaving like a child!" Grace burst out. She colored as one of the inn's guests walked down the hall to the parlor. Jimmy scowled again, and they waited in awkward silence until they were alone.

"What were you and Mike doing up there, anyway?" he asked, his cheeks red.

Grace evaded his question, guilty and ashamed in addition to being angry. "I think you owe him an apology," she said in a tight voice. "And you might have called first to see if I can go for a drive or not."

Jimmy walked heavily to a chair and lowered himself into it. "I'm sorry, I'm just . . ." He tried to hook the cane over the back of the chair, but it fell to the floor with a clatter. He swore under his breath.

A wave of pity and remorse swept aside Grace's anger. She set the punch bowl on a table and put one hand on his shoulder. Through his shirt, she felt how tense and rigid his muscles were. He was strung as tight as a bowstring.

"I'm sorry, too," she said. "I know it must be very hard for you."

Jimmy tipped his head to put his cheek against her hand. "Grace, sometimes I feel like I've lost everything."

"No. You haven't," she whispered. But as she looked over his head, down the corridor, she was filled with a terrible sense of loss herself. With an effort she made herself add, "You haven't lost me."

Light, quick footsteps sounded behind them. Nathan came trotting around the corner, and his eyes lit up when he saw Jimmy.

"Hi!" he said breathlessly. He planted himself in front of them, his face filled with admiration. "Tell me again how you shot the Nazis."

"Not now, kid." Jimmy turned his head away. "We're going out."

"Oh."

Grace knelt before a crestfallen Nathan and straightened his shirt. "Jimmy's feeling a little tired right now and his leg is hurting . . ." She winced as Jimmy made a restless, angry movement, but she kept her eyes on Nathan's. "Maybe later you can show him your model airplanes. How would that be?"

"Do you really want to see them?" Nathan asked, his face lighting up again.

"Sure, kid. Sure." Jimmy pushed himself out of the chair and grabbed his cane. "Come on, Grace."

With one more apologetic smile for Nathan, Grace

tucked her arm through Jimmy's and walked with him out to the car. She still had work to do, but she decided it was better to put it off, with Jimmy so upset. He was limping badly. She reached for the door handle to help him, and he gave her a fierce look.

"It's the man's job to open doors for ladies," he said.

Grace dropped her hand and followed him around to the other side of the car. He shifted his cane and opened the door. She got in without a word. His pride and his anger made her want to weep with pity. She loved him and yearned to help him. But she wasn't sure there was anything she could do.

They drove along the coast without speaking, the sun glittering on the wide ocean. As the silence stretched between them longer and longer, Grace felt even more that something terrible had happened, that something was lost never to be found again. She switched on the radio so that they would have an excuse for not talking. For a while, she kept her head turned to look out at the ocean, and the salty air streaming in through the window made her eyes water.

From some roadside stand in the distance, the smell of fried clams reached her on the wind. The scent filled Grace with bitter longing. She knew it was foolish to become sentimental over such a ridiculous thing. But on Jimmy's last night before he shipped overseas, he had taken her to a roadside fry-wagon for clams and shakes, and they had eaten together at a picnic bench and talked about what the future would bring them. Back then, there had been no doubt that the future would be golden and bright, but now Grace wondered how she could ever have been so young. It seemed to her now that they had been two entirely different people, in a different place, like the children in the home movie. And she couldn't see a way back.

After a while, Jimmy reached for her hand. She looked at him and managed a fleeting smile.

"This is a good song, isn't it?" he asked, nodding at the radio.

"Sure. It's nice."

"Remember how I taught you to dance?" Jimmy continued. "You stood on my feet."

Grace nodded, her throat so tight she wasn't sure she could speak. Involuntarily, she glanced down at his leg. Jimmy colored as he noticed her look.

"I guess you think I won't be doing much dancing, anymore."

"You will. I'm sure you will."

He laughed hollowly. "You're damned right I will. This is just temporary. Honest," he added, holding her gaze. "It's *all* just temporary."

Grace swallowed hard. With all her heart, she wanted to believe that. "I'm sure you're right."

Jimmy smiled and pulled the car off the road where it widened at a curve of the coast. They sat looking out at the breakers and the sailboats that cut across the water. The radio filled the awkwardness between them with careless dance tunes.

"Say, I've got good news," Jimmy spoke up at last.

Grace turned to him with relief. "Oh, good. What is it?"

"I called this buddy of mine," he said eagerly. "He's a bandleader, and he's going to bring a combo up from Boston. It's all arranged."

"What's all arranged?"

"For the party." Jimmy smiled. "You'll love it."

For a moment, Grace was too upset to answer him. She took a deep breath and switched off the radio. "Jimmy, you should have asked me first," she said calmly. "I've already spoken to some people about the music. I was going to make some more calls this afternoon."

"Well, now you don't need to," he said confidently. "I took care of it."

Grace was finding it hard not to let her anger show. She struggled to remain pleasant. "But how could you make plans without consulting me?"

He made an impatient gesture with one hand. "I don't see why it's so important. I'm just trying to help. And anyway, it's too late to cancel, and I wouldn't do it anyway. This guy's a buddy of mine."

"A buddy?" Grace's voice rose higher as she spoke. "A buddy is more important than me? You never even thought of asking what I wanted! It's my business, my party! You treat me like a child!" She was dangerously close to tears.

Jimmy gaped at her. His face was pale. "N-No I don't, Grace."

"You do," she said, roughly wiping her eyes with the back of her hand. "I don't feel as though you know me at all. Like we know each other at all. We're like strangers." She pressed her fist against her chin, utterly miserable.

"Grace," Jimmy whispered. "What are you saying? What do you mean?"

She sniffed and met his frightened gaze with a heavy heart. She wanted to reach out to him, but she couldn't bring herself to do it. "I don't know. I'm not sure what I mean, exactly, but you're not the boy I thought I knew, the boy I thought I would marry."

Out on the water, two sailboats steered toward each other, veering close and passing one another by. As the wind stiffened, the distance between the two boats grew.

"Grace, listen to me, please," Jimmy said in a tight voice. "I'm sorry. I know I've been kind of cranky with you."

"Not just me."

"Well, everyone, you, and Mike. And okay, Barbara, too," he added quickly. "Let me make it up to you. We'll all go to a club tomorrow night. How's that?"

"But you can't dance," Grace reminded him.

"You and Mike can dance," Jimmy said. "I'd enjoy just watching you. Honest. I want you to be friends, anyway. My best buddy and my best girl."

Grace looked through the windshield, seeing Mike as he'd been in the attic. "I think it would be better to do something alone," she said urgently. "Just you and me."

"No, don't be silly! I want to make it up to both of you," Jimmy said. "It'll be fun. You'll see."

"Jimmy—"

"No. Please." He took her hand. "I insist."

"You insist," she said in a flat voice.

He nodded quickly. "We'll have a swell time."

It was clear that he was anxious to please her; Grace's heart ached. She searched his face, wishing with all her soul that she could feel what she once felt. She was sure she loved him, but she was no longer sure whether she was *in* love with him.

"Well?"

With a painful smile, Grace nodded. "All right. As long as it's okay with Mike and Barb."

"Of course it will be," he said. He had a confident air, sure that Grace's feelings matched his own. He put the car into gear and made a U-turn. As they headed back into town, Jimmy regaled Grace with tales of Army life. She tried to pay attention, but instead found herself hoping that Mike would decline Jimmy's invitation.

She also hoped he wouldn't. Wincing, she slouched down in her seat and closed her eyes.

"I'll be in after dinner, to have a drink with the guys," Jimmy said as he dropped her off outside the Wild Rose. "They all want to hear my war stories."

"Good. See you later," Grace said. She started to open the door, and almost as an afterthought, turned back to kiss him good-bye.

He held her hand for a moment and looked into her eyes. "I love you, Grace. I hope you know that."

She nodded slowly. "I know."

Then she climbed out of the car. She stood watching as he drove away, and then entered the inn, deep in thought.

The Wild Rose was quiet, filled with the hush of late afternoon. Guests were in their rooms changing for dinner; her mother, the Teitelbaums and Sarah were no doubt in the kitchen and dining room, preparing the meal. Grace stood at the front desk, absently flicking one fingernail against the bell. It pinged faintly into the quiet of the lobby.

With an effort, she pulled herself together and strode purposefully to the dining room. She had responsibilities, duties, chores, she reminded herself. She needed to see that the hotel was running as it should.

"Where does this go?" came a teasing voice.

She stopped in the arched doorway. In the dining room Nathan was showing Mike how to set the tables. An unfolded napkin drooped from the little boy's hand; his starry eyes were on Mike.

"Like this?" Mike asked, draping the napkin over his head.

Nathan let out a peal of laughter. "No!"

"Like this?" Mike tied it around his neck like a bib.

"No!" Giggling, Nathan pointed to the table. "There."

Mike continued to tease Nathan, and Grace watched from the doorway. The dining room was filled with mellow, golden light, and the boy's bright laughter echoed off the walls like light bouncing off the water. Nathan tried to jump up and snatch the napkin from Mike's hand, but Mike was so tall that he could easily whisk it out of reach each time the giggling child leaped up. Then he pretended to drop his guard, and Nathan grabbed it with a cry of triumph. Over Nathan's head, Grace met Mike's eyes. He was full of life, full of affection for everyone and everything. Grace pictured him cheering a wounded soldier with the smile he was giving her now.

Then she heard a footstep behind her and turned, almost colliding with her mother. Mrs. MacKenzie grabbed Grace's arms to steady them both. "Whoa!"

"Sorry, Mom," Grace muttered, wiping a tear from the corner of her eye.

"What is it?"

Grace pulled away and brushed past her mother. "Nothing. It's nothing. It'll be a shame if he has to go back to the war, that's all."

She hurried off, leaving Mrs. MacKenzie frowning thoughtfully in the doorway.

Chapter Seven

"HOW ARE WE doing?" Grace asked in a brisk, businesslike voice as she entered the kitchen. She whisked an apron off its hook, tied it around her waist, and began lifting up pot lids, crashing and banging the covers of the pans. Steam rose into her face, adding to the tears on her lashes.

Rachel and Sarah stood watching her doubtfully. Grace seldom bothered to poke her nose into kitchen business before dinner, knowing that they always had everything under control. But she had to be busy and noisy and preoccupied. She couldn't think about Mike and the fact that he would soon return to the war.

"Everything looks fine." Grace opened one of the ovens and glanced at the biscuits browning inside. She couldn't get the picture of Mike's smile out of her mind. "Just fine, looks great."

"Thanks for checking up," Sarah said in her mildly

sarcastic way. She began whipping cream in a copper bowl, whistling softly along with the radio.

Grace stood wiping her hands on her apron and feeling like a fool. From the largest oven, the smell of roasting chickens was unbearably ordinary and routine. She gestured toward a heaping bowl of strawberries. "Shortcake on the menu tonight?"

"Mmmhmm," Sarah hummed. She met Rachel's eyes and quirked one blond eyebrow.

Nathan galloped into the kitchen and threw himself against his mother's knees with a shout. "Mama! Mama, can I go swimming with Mike tomorrow?"

"Of course, my darling," Rachel said. She rubbed the top of Nathan's head and smiled radiantly at Grace. "That Michael, such a nice boy."

"Oh, I guess he is," Grace replied. She yanked open the refrigerator door. Her back tingled. She wondered if Mike were about to follow Nathan into the kitchen.

"So kind, so patient with Nathan," Rachel went on. "What a good father he will make. A good husband, too. He says he'll become a doctor after the war."

"That doesn't necessarily mean he'd be a good husband," Grace said tartly. She slammed the refrigerator shut and turned with a ferocious scowl on her face. "Isn't there any cream? We can't serve strawberry shortcake without whipped cream."

"No, you're right," Sarah replied, looking up from her task. "Good thing I'm whipping it right now."

The color flooded into Grace's cheeks. She looked from Sarah to Rachel and back again, and then let out a weak laugh. "Maybe I should just leave you two to get on with business."

"Okie-dokie," Rachel sang.

For a moment, Grace stood gripping her hands together. She was thinking too much about Mike, and she knew it. She also knew she had to do something about it or she would go crazy. The most important task before her was to mend and care for her relationship with Jimmy, and that was going to be impossible until she took care of some business. Squaring her shoulders she turned and marched out of the kitchen to the dining room.

"Mike?" she called, her voice strong and determined. "Can I speak with you for a minute?"

"In here!"

She stepped into the dining room. Mike had set the tables and was standing in the center of the room, frowning over his work. His earnestness and desire to help filled Grace with an aching tenderness and made her almost weak in the knees.

"You didn't have to set the tables," she murmured. "That was so thoughtful of you."

Mike had one knife left over. He balanced it on the tip of one finger. "It's the least I can do," he said, his eyes on the knife. He let it drop, and caught it in midair and then took two more knives from the nearest table. As Grace watched with delight, he began to juggle the knives. They flashed brightly in the afternoon sun that slanted through the windows.

"Pretty tricky, huh?" he said, glancing at her with a wide smile. "When you're an orphan, you learn how to

94

entertain people. You're always trying to make everyone like you."

Grace put one hand to her cheek, a grin of pure joy on her face. "I can't believe you ever had any trouble that way."

"And I can recite poetry while I do it. 'There was an old lady of Fife, who juggled two plates and a knife'— Ahh!" Mike snatched the knives out of the air, one-two-three, and then swept her a low bow. "Ta-da!"

"Encore!" Grace applauded. She wanted to watch him forever.

"Now, what can I do for you?" he asked, setting the knives back on the table.

"Do?" Grace looked at him blankly, still smiling from ear to ear. Then she remembered, but she couldn't imagine what she could say that wouldn't sound like a lie.

"I have to talk to you," she began.

Mike pulled out a chair across from her and sat down. "Sure. Go ahead, I'm all ears."

More awkward than she had ever felt, Grace looked away from his smiling, open face. "I don't know how to say this."

"Just say it. You don't have to be shy or embarrassed with me," Mike said easily.

Grace was suddenly furious that he was so nice, so kind, so generous. "I love Jimmy very much," she said in a tight, emphatic voice. "I've always loved him. Ever since I was a little girl, you know."

"I know."

"And it's . . ." Grace had to look away again. She

kept her gaze on the blazing roses she could see through the window. "It's very important to me that he be happy, and that he have a good time. I'm not going to let anything upset him, because he's been through hell. Which you know perfectly well."

"Sure. I understand." Mike picked up one of the knives, then put it down again, clasped his hands together, and shifted on his chair.

Grace watched his nervous movements and thought she knew what prompted them. She wasn't the only one to feel the tension between them, but neither of them wanted to admit it, especially not Grace. She gritted her teeth.

"He's the sweetest, kindest—" Grace faltered. "He deserves for us to—"

"Sure," Mike broke in. He lowered his eyes. "I know."

"He wants to take us all out to a club tomorrow night, to go dancing," Grace pressed on grimly. "He wants us to be friends, and he'd like us to dance together, even though he can't, himself. And so, I think that, to please him, we should do what he wants."

Mike was so still and silent that finally Grace had to look up. He returned her gaze and didn't look away. Grace thought she might scream, or burst into tears. Both of them were trying to avoid saying the wrong thing, even though Grace was no longer sure what was right or wrong. She felt her hands shake, and pressed them more firmly together.

"If that's what you want," Mike said. "I'd be—only too happy to dance with you."

Grace scraped her chair back and made herself give Mike a false, bright smile. "Well, then it's settled. It would make Jimmy very happy. He's been through a terrible experience, and . . ." Her voice trailed off into nothing. She knew she was lying to herself and to Mike. And some reckless part of her prayed that he knew it, and that he would plead with her to stop.

But she made herself walk away from him, striding quickly out of the dining room. In the lobby she stopped and steadied herself against the reception desk. She touched the bell, and the guest register, and the pen placed in the crease of the book. Each of these objects was real and safe and as familiar as her own hands. Touching them was proof that some things were still the same, that some things wouldn't change.

Behind her, the door of the Wild Rose opened. When Grace turned, a telegram messenger was just stepping into the lobby. Her heart made a terrible lurch, but she kept her hands behind her back. "Yes?"

"Telegram for MacKenzie," the boy said, snapping his gum.

Grace stared at the envelope, but couldn't make herself reach for it.

"Miss?"

At the same moment, Mrs. MacKenzie came waltzing down the main staircase. "Gracie, Gracie do you know what I've been thinking just—"

She stopped when she saw the messenger, and the airy smile vanished from her face. "What is it?"

"Telegram for MacKenzie," the boy repeated impatiently.

Grace and her mother looked at one another, and together, walked forward to take the telegram. Mrs. MacKenzie gave the boy a quarter. "Thank you."

Only when they were alone again did Grace's mother slide her thumb under the flap of the envelope. Her hands were steady as she drew out the slip of paper. Grace felt her heart beating like a kettle drum in her ears. They put their heads together to read.

"USS *CARL TAYLOR* TORPEDOED STOP HEAVY CASUALTIES STOP I'M FINE STOP DON'T WORRY STOP LOVE YOU BOTH STOP BOB"

Mrs. MacKenzie folded the telegram very carefully and put it back in the envelope. Her face was ashy white.

"He's fine, Mom," Grace said in a hoarse voice. "Dad's fine."

Her mother put one hand over her eyes and stood there, swaying slightly. "Let him come back. Please, God. Bring him back."

"The war will be over soon, it has to be," Grace said with far more conviction than she felt. "He'll come home soon. And Mark, too."

"God, you'd better be right," Mrs. MacKenzie said shakily. "I don't know how much longer I can stand this waiting." Slowly, she crumpled the telegram in her fist and began to cry. "I love your father so much."

Grace pulled her mother into a hug and held her tight. She began to cry, too. She cried that she no longer had to wait for the man she loved to come home from the war. And she cried because her heart felt as though it were being dragged from her by force.

Chapter Eight

"I HAVE AN announcement," Barbara said the next day as she took a chair in the workers' lounge of the factory. She waited until all eyes were on her. "I'm going to trade in my typewriter for a welding mask."

Grace set her coffee cup down and gaped at her friend. "What?"

Helen Diggory, who was one of the packers, broke into ironic applause. "Rosie the Riveter, in the flesh."

"Thank you, thank you, glad to be among you," Barbara said with a bow.

"But why?" asked a young woman named Patty, for whom everything was a wonderment. She looked at Barbara as if she'd sprouted wings.

"The money's much much better," Barbara explained. "Do you know what kind of wage they pay at the dockyards?" She rolled her eyes. "Enormous, compared to what they pay secretaries."

"But which dockyard?" Grace asked. "Boston? Isn't that far to go for a job?"

"So what?" Barbara shrugged. "With the extra money I make, I'll buy a car. Until then I'll take the bus."

The other women around the table looked as though they knew exactly how Barbara felt. "Honey, if I were you, I'd do it too," Helen said. "But I get seasick even in drydock."

Grace laughed with the others. The women who worked at the plant were young and old, fat and thin, from all over Marblehead and the surrounding towns of Cape Ann. As different as they all were, the one thing they shared was a sense of camaraderie. They were doing men's jobs, and they knew they were doing them well. For some, it was the first job they'd ever held outside the home, and all of them had a strong sense of accomplishment.

"My husband wrote me a letter the other day," said a middle-aged brunette named Gladys. She leaned across the table and sent a long look around it. "He wants to know if I'm still ironing the sheets. Stuck in a lousy fuel depot in France and all he can think about is how nice I used to iron the sheets. Can't wait to come home to that."

Helen giggled. "What are you going to tell him?"

"I'll tell him that when I get home from canning fish all day, I buy food, feed the kids, pay the bills, water the garden, wash the clothes, clean the house, check on my aging mother, and then sometime around midnight, as I drop into bed, I think—gosh, maybe I should iron the sheets."

"And then she says, 'Nah,' " Barbara said.

"Amen to that, sister." Gladys picked up her coffee cup and toasted the group with it.

"Imagine him thinking you have time to iron sheets these days," Grace said, laughing.

Barbara gave her a sly look. "I bet Jimmy's mom irons the sheets."

Grace picked up a bottle cap and lobbed it at her friend. "Well, she doesn't work at a fish factory all day."

"I guess that means she doesn't smell like a cod," Helen observed. She sniffed her shirtsleeve and made a face. "P-U."

Gladys put a hand on Grace's arm and smiled maternally. "Now, how is that nice Jimmy? Are you two making wedding plans yet?"

"She's too busy practicing her ironing," Barbara put in.

Patty's eyes widened. "You are? Oh, she's teasing," she gasped. "Grace, are you going to have a big wedding with a white dress and everything?"

"Oh, well I suppose so," Grace murmured vaguely.

"My wedding was nothing like I planned it," Gladys sighed. "I always wanted to elope. Imagine how romantic. No formal plans, no fussing. Just pure romance."

"That's not going to do for Grace," Helen said. She stretched widely. "When a MacKenzie and a Penworthy get married, that calls for an enormous wedding. Grace is already related to half the town, and Jimmy's related to the other half, and once they get married all of Marblehead will be one huge family."

102

"Sickening, isn't it?" Barbara joked. "Two of the oldest families in town. Positively feudal."

"But we'll still invite all you Johnny-come-latelies whose families didn't come to America until after the Revolution," Grace said with a toss of her head. "*If* you're nice."

Helen put her hands together in prayer. "Oh, please, please please. I'll be ever so good and I won't steal the silver."

"Don't you pay any attention to their teasing," Gladys said, patting Grace's arm. "We're all very happy and excited for you."

"Thanks." Grace sipped her coffee, and made a show of getting a stray coffee ground off the rim so she could keep her eyes down.

"What a lovely thing to look forward to," Helen said, all sarcasm aside. "And they say the Penworthys are well-off. You won't have to work anymore."

"I don't really have to work now," Grace said defensively. "I wanted the accounting experience and more importantly, I wanted to do my share for the war effort. I enjoy working. Maybe I won't quit until I take over the Wild Rose full-time."

"I know someone who won't like that," Barbara said in a singsong.

Patty looked astonished, as usual. "Who?"

Grace scowled at Barbara. "Cut it out. Jimmy's not going to tell me what to do."

"Good." Barbara gave Grace a sweet smile. "I'm very glad to hear that."

Groaning, Grace dropped her head into her hands. "You're too much, Barb. Jimmy won't be my boss, just get that notion out of your mind."

"All right," Barbara said. She turned to Helen. "Let's make a bet. I've got five dollars says he'll ask her to quit. Want some of the action?"

Helen frowned at Barbara. "I think that's enough, now, Barbie."

"I don't mind what she says," Grace said, even as she told herself that Barbara would win the bet. She smiled at her friend. "No hard feelings."

Barbara grimaced. "Sorry."

Grace stirred her coffee, smiling distantly at the others. Mike would never think of asking her to quit her job, she was sure of that. He understood why she liked working at a smelly, noisy fish factory. Almost from the moment she had met him, she had felt that he could read her thoughts.

"Somebody's daydreaming," Gladys said with a knowing smile.

Grace's spoon rattled against the cup. "No, I wasn't," she stammered, alarmed to find her thoughts had strayed to Mike again.

"When a girl's in love, there's no hiding it," Patty said dreamily. "She's thinking about her fella."

"But . . ." Grace opened and shut her mouth. She couldn't insist that she wasn't in love, because the women assumed she had been thinking of Jimmy. The futility and foolishness of it all made her shake her head in despair.

"Are you going to start a family right away?" Helen asked.

"Oh, I—I—" Grace stammered. "I don't know."

"What does Jimmy want? A big family?" Gladys leaned forward, watching Grace's every expression.

"I think he—I thought I'd wait," Grace mumbled, unable to meet the woman's eyes.

"I think you're so lucky," Patty went on. "The man you love is a real true hero, just like in the pictures."

"I'll tell you something," Helen said, pointing her finger at everyone and no one. "I'd rather do anything than have to lead soldiers against a machine-gun nest. What could be more terrifying than that?"

"He must be a true leader," Gladys agreed. "My husband, on the other hand, is a natural-born follower."

"Well, at least that's a safe place to be," Helen teased kindly. "The Third Army is so big, by the time the end of the column catches up with the front, the war will be over."

Gladys chuckled and retied her red kerchief around her hair. "That's fine with me. I don't need a hero, I just need my husband back. Grace can be the one with the hero."

"Do you suppose he'll run for mayor? He'd probably win hands down, folks are so proud of him," Helen speculated.

Grace didn't add to the conversation. And she noticed that Barbara didn't speak, either. The two friends looked at each other in silence as Patty, Helen, and Gladys traded observations about Jimmy's heroism. With every word spoken, Grace felt more and more out of place. She knew she should say something, should add her voice to theirs and boast and be proud, but she couldn't.

Behind her, the door of the break room opened. Grace turned with a grateful smile, glad to be spared the need to say something about Jimmy. Mr. Tedisco, the plant manager, stepped in, and the expression on his face made Grace suddenly anxious. The women in the room all turned to look at him, smiling expectantly. But their smiles faded as he beckoned to Gladys.

"Mrs. Ledue, I need to speak to you," he said solemnly.

Ashen, Gladys stood up and walked stiffly across the room. Mr. Tedisco ushered her out and shut the door.

At the table, there was a dread-filled silence. Grace twisted her hands together in her lap, fearing the worst. An urgent summons in the middle of the working day was never an occasion for joy; on the contrary, it was always the worst kind of news.

From the hallway there came an anguished cry, and then broken sobs. "God, no!" Gladys wailed. "No, NO!"

Grace covered her eyes with one hand.

"I guess she won't need to iron those sheets now," Helen said in a tearful voice.

Barbara pushed her chair back. "I'll take her home."

Patty began to cry, tears running unchecked down her pale face. "I had three brothers, you know. Three. They're all gone. When's the war going to be over?"

Grace felt as though she were being strangled. "I don't know," she whispered. "God, I don't know."

The sound of Gladys's hysterical sobs grew fainter, and out on the water, a ship's horn blasted harsh and sour. Weak with pity, Grace went back to the business office. And each time she pulled the handle of the adding machine, she had the horrible notion that she was toting up an endless sum of deaths.

Grace walked home from work, glad for the chance to be by herself. The lowering sun laid a sheet of light across the water as she tramped toward town, and on her left the cliffs dropped down to the ocean. Gulls wheeled up from below, rising on the updrafts from the water as the air cooled, and shrieking like lost souls. Grace paused for a moment, facing the ocean, narrowing her eyes against the horizon.

Even in her wildest dreams, she couldn't imagine a more beautiful scene, a more perfect spot. The Atlantic coast was wild and beautiful, and the ocean stretched magnificently as far as the eye could see. Sailboats plied the water as calmly as if there were no war; the distant beach smoked with picnic fires; sandpipers raced along the sand and flew crying into the salt spray. All was peace and tranquillity and safety. And yet the war that snarled and snaked and lashed its tail around the world could reach out and drive an arrow into a woman's heart as she laughed with her friends.

From nearby there were shrieks and calls that weren't made by gulls. Grace turned around and saw a gang of boys scrambling up the cliffs. They waved sticks in their hands and shouted urgent military commands. Grace was startled to see Nathan tagging along behind them.

"Nathan!"

The little boy stopped and looked yearningly as the bigger boys ran on ahead. Grace beckoned to him. He trudged toward her with reluctance written all over his face. Grace took him by the arms.

"What are you doing playing on these rocks?" she asked him sternly. "This is a very dangerous place."

"I'm not afraid," Nathan declared. He struggled out of her grip and picked up the stick he had dropped. "I'm going to be like Jimmy."

Grace flinched as though he had threatened her with the stick. "What do you mean, like Jimmy?"

"This is the beach of Normandy, and I'm killing Nazis," Nathan yelled. "I'm going to shoot them!"

He dodged away from her and took up a firing stance. "Bang! Bang!" His childish shouts were whisked away by the wind. He stood defiantly on the edge of the land, shooting a whole ocean full of enemies.

Grace went cold as she watched him in his make-believe. She ran after him, took him firmly by the arm, and dragged him back from the cliff side. "You're not to play soldiers," she cried passionately. "Don't play war, it's not a game!"

"You can't stop me!" The little boy tried to wriggle out of her grip, but Grace held on tight. "Let go! I'll shoot you!"

Stunned, Grace dropped his arm and stared at him in dismay.

"Nathan, you're being very naughty and you should be ashamed to speak to me that way." She tried not to shake, but she found her hands trembling. "Nathan, come home with me right now."

Nathan ran several steps and spun around to face her. His round face was flushed with excitement. "I'm going to be a brave fighter like Jimmy! When I'm grown to be a man, I will go to the war."

Grace's voice stuck in her throat. "This war will be over before you are a man, Nathan."

"No! No, I will fight!" He whirled around and chased after the pack of boys scrambling among the rocks. "Bang! Bang!"

Still trembling, Grace hugged her arms around herself and watched him join his playmates at the edge of the Atlantic. The wind from the east carried their battle cries to her, almost as if they were the cries and screams of the men fighting in France.

Chapter Nine

AT SEVEN-THIRTY, GRACE descended to the lobby of the Wild Rose, her taffeta skirt whispering faintly. Mike was sitting in an armchair, flipping through *Stars and Stripes,* but he leaped to his feet when he saw her. Neither of them spoke for a moment. Grace saw him look at her dress, her hair, the locket at her throat. She fussed with the clasp of her purse.

"Ready?" she asked in a low voice.

He nodded. "I guess Jimmy will be here in a minute."

They stood awkwardly by the reception desk, avoiding each other's gaze. Mike was in dress uniform, his hat tucked under his arm. He ran one finger under his collar, and glanced again at Grace.

"You look swell."

"Thank you." She looked up, and their eyes met. Grace felt her heartbeat quicken.

Mike was silent and stood with his hat in his hands,

staring stonily at the floor. "Party plans coming along okay?" he asked.

"Yes, fine, thank you," Grace replied in a formal voice. She closed her eyes for a moment, wishing helplessly that the evening could be canceled.

Outside, a car honked.

"That must be him," Mike said.

Grace hurried ahead of him out of the inn. Jimmy was holding open the car door for her, and she ducked in with a breathless hello. Barbara was already in the backseat.

"Hi," Grace said.

"Hi yourself, kiddo."

Barbara patted her hair into place, her eyes on the rearview mirror. She still looked drawn and depressed over Gladys's tragedy, but she smiled as Mike climbed in beside her. Jimmy took his place at the wheel. He was wearing his dress uniform, too, as his old civilian clothes were too boyish, and he looked handsome and proud. But Grace told herself with a rush of guilt that Mike suited his uniform better.

"Everyone ready for a good time?" Jimmy asked in a hearty voice.

"Sure," Barbara said dryly.

"We're going to a joint up in Salem," Jimmy went on cheerfully. "I hear it's really swinging."

"Isn't that where they had the witches?" Mike asked in a distant voice.

"One of my ancestors was accused of witchcraft,"

111

Grace answered with forced nonchalance. "She had to get out of town, fast. She ended up in Nova Scotia."

"Some of my great-great-greats were around back then, too." Jimmy launched into a long, complicated story about their family trees, and Grace stared out the window at the dusk. She could almost feel Mike watching her from the backseat, but she made herself concentrate on the scenery. She counted mailboxes, dogs, flags, anything to blot out all sense and knowledge of Mike behind her. Jimmy turned to her suddenly.

"Wasn't it your great-great-grandfather who sold the land that my family ended up putting the Ford dealership on?"

"I don't remember." Grace tried to puzzle out the chronology, desperate for something to take her mind off Mike. She felt dizzy.

"Jeez," Barbara spoke up. "I'm glad you guys will even talk to me, even though my folks didn't come over on the *Mayflower*."

"Let's not start this again," Grace begged. She turned around and gave Barbara a pleading look, carefully avoiding looking at Mike. She could see him from the corner of her eye, though.

Jimmy pulled the car into the parking lot of the nightclub. He angled around in the front seat, extending one hand to Barbara. "Truce?"

"Sure. Why not?" Barbara shook Jimmy's hand.

"We're all going to have a swell time tonight, I insist," Jimmy said. He smiled blissfully at Grace. "And you look so pretty every guy here is going to turn pea-green with envy."

Grace blushed uncomfortably. "No, they won't."

"Doesn't she look incredible, Mike?" Jimmy asked.

"Sure. So does Barbara," Mike agreed, his eyes on Grace.

Barbara rolled her eyes and linked arms with Grace and the two of them headed for the entrance. "If I stick close to you, maybe some of your leftovers will ask me to dance."

"Barbie," Grace whispered, stealing a quick look over her shoulder. Jimmy and Mike were coming along more slowly, deep in conversation and gesturing with their hands. "Do me a favor," she begged.

"What? You name it."

"Could you please dance most of the dances with Mike?"

Barbara smiled knowingly. "Are you trying to set us up? Because although it's very sweet of you, I already told you—"

"He's not your type, I know," Grace said.

Their eyes met. As the distant beat of dance music reached them from inside, Barbara's smile faded. "But he's yours."

Grace couldn't answer. Jimmy and Mike joined them, and Mike opened the door. "After you, ladies."

Inside, Jimmy waved down the maître d' and opened his arms expansively. "The best table for me and my friends," he said.

"Of course. Nothing is too good for our men in uniform," the man said with a bow. "Please. Follow me."

Grace and Barbara went ahead of the men into the glamorous ballroom of the club. A big band was playing a rollicking swing number, and couples whirled around the dance floor in a dazzle of party dresses, uniforms, and tuxedos. Grace wove her way among the crowded tables, clutching her purse like a life preserver. The head waiter led them to a round table against the wall, and Grace and Barbara slid into the banquette, their stiff dresses rustling across the leather.

"Is this great or what?" Jimmy clapped his hands together and winked as another waiter sidled up to their table. "Champagne all around. I feel like celebrating tonight."

"Very good, sir."

Grace raised her head and forced a smile. "This is a lovely place, Jimmy. Thanks for bringing us."

"Nothing's too good for you, sweetheart," he replied, putting his hand over hers. He kissed her cheek.

Even while Jimmy's lips still touched her face, Grace automatically sought Mike's eyes across the table. He was fingering the bud vase, and for a moment, he looked up at her.

"Hey, how about a dance?" Barbara said brightly, glancing from Grace to Mike. She nudged him with her elbow. "Come on, big boy. Spin me around the floor."

"I'd love to," he replied, instantly standing up.

Grace couldn't help watching as they left for the dance floor. Mike took Barbara in his arms and led her among the dancers. He was the tallest man there, and Grace had no trouble keeping him in sight. Beyond the swirling crowd, she could see him clearly, smiling at Barbara.

"I said you're really beautiful tonight, Grace."

Startled, she looked at Jimmy. He was smiling at her, and he touched her cheek with one finger.

"Just beautiful," he repeated.

"Thanks."

He picked up two champagne glasses and handed one to her. "Before they get back, let's drink a toast by ourselves. To us."

Grace raised her glass and smiled painfully. "To happy days."

When they clinked the glasses together, Grace had a frightening sensation that she herself was made of glass and might shatter at the slightest touch. As she sipped her champagne, she watched Jimmy and tried to remember loving him. She wanted so much to love him that tears of grief came to her eyes.

"Hey, what is it?" he asked tenderly.

"Nothing, I'm fine," Grace lied. She sipped more champagne and waved one hand before her nose. "It's the bubbles."

Barbara and Mike returned to the table as a singer in a long, sequined black gown walked out onto the stage. There was enthusiastic applause, and the woman bowed regally.

"Why don't you two dance," Jimmy said, motioning to Mike and Grace.

She shrank back against the leather seat. "Oh, I don't know if—"

"Go on, go on," Jimmy said with a laugh.

Near panic, Grace turned to Barbara, who snapped her fingers. "Say, Mike could you get me some cigarettes?"

But Mike stood up, holding his hand out to Grace. "Our host wants us to dance, I guess we should oblige."

He never took his eyes off Grace as he spoke, and she found herself unable to say no. Almost in a trance, she put her hand in his and let him lead her away from the table. Jimmy smiled and waved as they left.

The music began soft and slow, the drummer brushing the snares with a gentle whisper like rain, and the piano picking out the Cole Porter chords. As the singer stepped up to the microphone, Mike put his hand on Grace's waist, and she put hers on his shoulder. She didn't dare look at him.

"Get out of town, before it's too late, my love," the song began.

The singer's voice was low and sultry, and she held the microphone as though caressing a lover's face. Grace felt Mike's hand through her dress, and his breath was warm against her neck. She closed her eyes.

"Just disappear, I care for you much too much." The singer seemed to be whispering right in her ear.

All around them, couples were dancing close, their bodies touching, their feet hardly moving to the seductive melody. Mike pulled Grace closer and rested his cheek against her hair. She put her cheek to his shoulder and felt a shiver go up her spine as he twined his fingers with hers.

"Grace," Mike whispered.

She lifted her head. They stared at one another as the lyrics ended in a sigh.

"What are we doing?" Grace asked, tears glistening in her eyes.

He looked stricken with guilt. "I don't know. I'm sorry."

The music ended at last, and the audience broke into wild applause. But Grace and Mike stayed in each other's arms.

"May I have this dance?" an older man asked, making a courtly, old-fashioned bow to Grace.

She blinked the tears away, trying to pull herself into the present. "Oh, why I—"

"Excuse me," Mike said. He backed away.

With a smile frozen on her face, Grace let the old gentleman waltz her around the room, and somehow managed to find polite answers to his small talk. But her thoughts were spinning as fast as the dancers were, and every time she turned, she saw Jimmy and Mike seated side by side, their faces passing in a blur. At last the waltz was over, and Grace excused herself with breathless thanks.

She made her way back to the table, willing herself not to search for Mike's gaze. They looked at each other in spite of themselves, but Grace made herself smile weakly at Jimmy.

"He was an old dear," she explained quickly. "I couldn't say no to him."

"You were swell to dance with him," Jimmy said.

Barbara shook a cigarette out of a pack and held it to her lips. "How about a light, someone?"

Without expression, Mike reached into his pocket and drew out a Zippo. He flicked it open for Barbara, and then snapped it shut. His face was as rigid as a mask.

"I have an announcement," he said abruptly.

Grace's heart plunged. For one wild moment, she thought he was going to say something about them. Her imagination raced.

"I'm going back to France. They need medics and I've got to go."

At first, Grace thought she had gone deaf. The music faded and there was a buzzing in her ears. She stared at Mike, speechless.

"And let me make a toast to both of you," Mike continued. He raised his glass to Grace and Jimmy. "You're a wonderful couple and you deserve the best."

Tears came to Grace's eyes. She couldn't check them. They spilled over her cheeks and onto the white tablecloth.

"Grace, honey!" Jimmy exclaimed.

Stricken, Grace fumbled in her purse for a handkerchief. She couldn't see.

With a sob she pushed away from the table and ran blindly toward a waiter. "The ladies' room?"

"That way, miss," he said with a sweeping gesture.

She hurried into the lounge, crying bitterly, and

flung herself into a chair before the mirror. Still fumbling in her purse, she emptied the contents onto the makeup table. Lipstick, comb, compact, wallet—everything cascaded to the floor and scattered. Grace put her face in her hands and sobbed.

Behind her the door opened and shut. Grace felt a warm hand on her shoulder.

"Oh, Barb, I've lost everything!" Grace wailed. "Everything!"

"We can pick it up, honey, just—"

"No, you don't understand," Grace broke in wildly. She pressed her fingers against her eyes until she saw stars behind her lids. It hurt terribly. "I can't marry Jimmy. I don't love him anymore. What'll I do? I can't go through with it."

"What a mess." Gently, Barbara drew Grace's hands away from her face and wiped her tears with a handkerchief. "There's only one thing to do. You have to tell him."

"But he's been through so much!" Grace shook her head. "How can I hurt him even more? It'll break his heart."

Barbara frowned. For once, her hard-bitten, ironic manner was tender. "Listen, honey. You can't marry a man you don't love. You'll break your own heart that way. Don't kid yourself that you'd be making a sacrifice for him, because he'll be miserable. You can't hide an empty heart from him forever."

"Oh, God," Grace whispered. She bent to pick up her scattered things from the floor, and arranged them

119

carefully on the vanity: compact, lipstick, comb, wallet. It was a pity her life couldn't be so easily ordered. She sniffed. "After what he went through in the war, it's just so unfair."

To her surprise, Barbara laughed, a short, rueful chuckle. "Well, if that doesn't beat all. They do say all's fair in love and war. You've got love and war here, there's not a damn thing fair about any of it."

Grace hugged herself and shivered. "I don't know what to do."

"Yes, you do, kid," Barbara said, smoothing Grace's hair and looking earnestly into her eyes. "You know what you have to do, and you know no one is going to do it for you."

"I know."

From out in the club there was a drum roll and a burst of applause. The excitement and gaiety outside only made Grace feel more alone.

"I think I need a few minutes by myself," she whispered. She kissed Barbara's cheek. "Thanks for being such a pal."

"Are you going to be okay?" her friend asked.

Grace sniffled again and blew her nose. "No. Not right away."

With a sigh Barbara stood up and left the lounge. Grace put her elbows on the vanity and gazed mournfully at her reflection. She had wanted so much to grow up, to take on the responsibilities of the inn and the job at the factory. She had chafed when Jimmy treated her like a child, but now that she was faced with a bitter duty, she wanted more than anything to be that child again who had adored Jimmy so much.

Because it wasn't just that Jimmy had changed, Grace realized. She had grown up, and left behind that starry-eyed girl who had idolized him. There was no use pretending they would ever recapture those feelings. There was no use lying to herself or Jimmy any longer.

Grace swept her belongings into her purse and went back out to the club. As she neared the table, she saw Jimmy sitting by himself, toying with the stem of his champagne glass.

"Are Mike and Barbara dancing?" she asked in a low, dispirited voice.

"They left," Jimmy said. "Barbara had a headache, so Mike took her home in a cab."

"Oh." Grace felt her shoulders sag, as though the last shred of her strength had drained away. Now nothing prevented her from telling Jimmy the bad news except her own cowardice. She raised her eyes slowly, and found him smiling at her. "What is it?"

"I'm so happy," he said, taking her hand and smoothing her fingers across his palm. "You got so emotional when Mike made that toast to us, I figured that meant you'd forgiven me. You have, right? And we are going to get married, like we always said we would?"

Grace didn't understand how her heart could possibly feel even more pain than it had already. "I have forgiven you."

"So maybe at the party we could make an announce-ment?" he pressed on eagerly.

"Oh, Jimmy. I've forgiven you, but I . . ." Grace's throat closed on the words. She turned her head away, fighting for courage.

"But you what?"

She drew a harsh breath. "I can't marry you, Jimmy. I'm so sorry."

He stared at her, dumbfounded, and the color drained from his face and quickly flooded in again. He was still holding her hand, gripping it hard, so hard her fingers ached. "What? But I thought—"

"We both thought a lot of things," Grace broke in. "But I think we both know this isn't right."

Jimmy began shaking his head. "No, I know no such thing. Has Barbara been turning you against me? Is that what went on with you two in the ladies' room?"

"No, Jimmy, no." Grace eased her hand out of his. "It has nothing to do with her or—or anyone," she stammered.

He leaned across the table, his expression passionate and angry. "Or who? What does that mean? Were you seeing someone while I was gone?"

"No!"

"Maybe spending time with a healthy specimen like Mike gave you second thoughts, is that it? He likes you enough, that's obvious. You can do a lot better than a shot-up wreck like me."

Grace cringed, in an agony of embarrassment. Couples at tables within earshot were looking their way. Grace

122

lowered her voice. "Jimmy, please don't make this any harder—"

"I'm making this hard?"

"Jimmy, *please*. I'm not the same person you left behind, and you're not the same person I said good-bye to. Let's give up pretending this is three years ago."

Jimmy sat back heavily against the banquette, shaking his head. "Oh, this is rich. So rich. All those guys that got dear John letters when we were overseas, and I was so smug about you."

"Don't . . ." Grace begged.

"I survive D-Day and get shot in the heart in my own backyard. Very ironic, don't you think, Grace?"

She was shaking. A waiter hovered nearby, wringing his hands.

"May I bring anything, sir?" the man asked nervously.

"We don't need anything," Jimmy snapped.

"Don't do this, Jimmy. Let's go home."

"I guess I can't blame you for not wanting to get stuck with a cripple," he continued with a sneer. "I wouldn't be much good to you in your precious bar. Well, I'm sorry, I was serving my country instead of serving drinks."

Grace recoiled. "I've been serving my country, too," she said tightly.

"Oh, please, Grace. Don't embarrass yourself." He turned his head deliberately away from her.

Tears stung her eyes. She couldn't believe it was ending in such a horrible scene. With trembling hands, she

123

picked up her purse and her wrap and stood up. "I'm going to take a cab home."

He still didn't turn to look at her. He drummed his fingers on the top of the banquette.

Grace watched him in miserable silence for a moment, and then turned and left.

Chapter Ten

TOWARD DAWN, AFTER a long and bitter night of staring at the ceiling, Grace fell into a troubled sleep. In her dream, she was sitting in a swing, rising higher and higher into the blue sky as someone pushed her. Birds sang among the treetops, and the leafy boughs rustled their branches together, whispering like secret lovers. The hands that caught her waist and pushed her with each fall of the swing were warm and strong, and Grace felt happiness overtake her as she reached for the sky.

"Oh, Jimmy, I'm so glad you came back at last," she said.

She turned around with an ecstatic smile, but it was Mike pushing her. Her heart raced with fear and excitement and surprise, and she gripped the swing.

"Not so high!" she pleaded. "I'll fall!"

Mike smiled, his brown eyes flecked with prairie gold. "Don't worry. You're safe with me!"

But Grace panicked, and she sat bolt upright in bed. She could hear her heart knocking against her ribs. Through the open window she heard the first drowsy stirrings of the birds, and the eastern sky was pale gray.

"Oh, God," she groaned, putting her face in her hands.

She knew it was no use trying to sleep. And besides, the thought of falling into another dream filled her with alarm.

Grace dressed quickly, stepping into jeans and shrugging on a sweatshirt. She tiptoed out into the hall. The Wild Rose Inn and all its lodgers still slept quietly. With one yearning look down the hall to Mike's room, Grace ran down the stairs and out the front door.

Without thinking of what she did, Grace hurried up Front Street. A cat slinking home from a night prowl stopped and stared at her and then hurried away as Grace ran past. Full milk bottles sat on doorsteps, the cream a heavy yellow layer at the top, drops of condensation slipping down their sides like tears. A solitary sparrow, brown and plain, poked around in the gutter. Grace cut through an alley, making her way gradually uphill. Beneath an elm tree she stopped to catch her breath and take stock.

She was at the bottom of Burial Hill. Often, in her childhood, she had climbed up among the graves with her brother and Jimmy, hunting their ancestors. "Got one! Here's another!" they would call, their childish voices bouncing full of life among the dead.

Grace followed the path up with her eyes. Stretching

away on either side were countless graves of MacKenzies and Carters, Trelawneys, Handys, and Bulls—and Penworthys. What so many people had wished for, that the MacKenzies and Penworthys would be united after three centuries—would never happen, now. Grace bowed her head, wondering if the ancient dead knew, and if they cared.

Sighing, she stepped off the sidewalk and onto the grass-edged path. Among the lichened stones were too many fresh ones, with American flags poked into the new-dug earth. There were boys Grace had known from infancy, fathers and uncles and cousins. And there were girls and women, too, the ones who had trained as nurses and saved lives before giving their own, and the recruits of the Women's Air Corps and the other military services.

Gave his life for his country, the stones read. *Fallen in battle on foreign soil.*

Grace's footsteps slowed as she climbed the rocky hill. The war was too greedy. *How many more men and women did it want?* she asked herself sadly.

At the top, she sat against a gravestone and hugged her knees. Part of her heart should be there, too, she mused. And something of Jimmy. He had risked his life for his country and survived, but not intact. Some wounds went deeper than skin and flesh and cut pieces from the heart. The better part of Jimmy had fallen on the beaches of Normandy, Grace mourned silently. His heart, his golden nature, his spirit.

She bowed her head to her folded arms. It was a

terrible, greedy war, a hungry war, reaching across the globe and eating everyone it touched.

And Mike was returning to it.

Grace shuddered. Between her knees, she saw the short grasses and lichen that grew on that rocky hill. And as she watched, their shadows stretched behind them. She looked up, squinting against the rising sun. The light spread across the tops of houses out on Marblehead Neck, across the harbor and the roofs of town, over the green crowns of the trees below her. That sun had already seen France today, Grace realized, had already illuminated many more deaths.

She dropped her gaze, and saw a man begin climbing the path down below her, and in a moment of dizzy joy, she recognized Mike. She held her breath, praying that he had followed her, hoping that he hadn't. He was going back to war, and she knew she was so in love with him that her heart would die if he did. What a bitter irony it was, that Jimmy had returned from the war with a friend who was everything he once was: kind, gentle, and generous.

And yet Mike was something more than Jimmy ever had been. Mike had never known her as a child, and only saw her for who and what she was. Grace wanted to call out to him, but something held her back. She almost feared he would hear her heart, although she made no sound.

But he was walking with his head bowed, slowly, meandering among the graves. He didn't see her. He seemed to be searching, and he stopped from time to time

128

to read an inscription, and touch a stone. With a wrenching tug at her heart, she realized he sought MacKenzie graves. She knew the place of each one, and he found them one at a time, kneeling and learning them. He was the orphan, searching for a family of his own. Grace thought she would cry with love for him.

He came within yards of her before he looked up. Then their eyes met across the short distance. Neither of them spoke. His throat moved as he swallowed, and he touched the top of the marker for David MacKenzie, Grace's grandfather who had died in World War I.

"They called this the Great War," he said hoarsely.

Grace shook her head in pain. "How can any war be great?"

He didn't answer, and Grace stood as though someone were pulling her. Without another word, she ran down to him and he caught her in his arms.

"Grace, my God, I love you so much," he whispered, kissing her throat and her mouth and her eyes. "What will I do?"

"Just hold me," she sobbed. She didn't know if she was crying from fear or joy, but she knew she couldn't do anything but cling to him.

"I hate myself for loving you," he said roughly. "I didn't want to, I tried so hard not to. I'm such a traitor."

"No. No." She looked up at him, touching his lips with trembling fingers. "I'm not marrying Jimmy. I told him last night."

"You did?" Mike held her face in his hands and searched her eyes. "God, what have we done?"

"I don't know." She buried her face in his shoulder, her heart so full that she thought she would burn into nothing and be flung away on the wind.

"Grace." He kissed her hair. "Tell me you love me."

With a sob, she wrenched away from him and held herself against a gravestone. "I won't. I can't promise myself to a soldier again."

He followed her and wrapped his arms around her. She leaned back against him, shaking her head. The leaves of the treetops whispered and the birds darted in and out among them, singing into the blue sky. It was so much like her dream that it made her want to weep. She knew she was feeling what she had always seen in her mother and been frightened by: a passion so strong it made everything else seem like nothing.

"I can't say I love you," she said. "I can't make any promises. Not out loud."

Mike turned her around in his arms and gripped her shoulders. "Not out loud."

"No."

They looked into one another's eyes, shaking with emotion. Grace could not believe how terrible and strong the feeling was.

"Not out loud," he repeated, his voice tender as he brought her hands to his lips. He kissed her palms, and then her fingers as Grace looked at the top of his head. She had to close her eyes against the sun.

They stood embracing as the day brightened around them. Then Mike pulled back and smiled into her face. He laughed.

"This is incredible," he said wonderingly.

She smiled, suddenly shy. "I know. But I'm afraid."

"Don't worry," he said. "You're safe with me."

Grace winced and broke away from him. "I—I'm not sure I believe that," she said with difficulty. "But let's not think about the future."

"But—"

"No. No promises," she pleaded. "Let's just be happy right now."

Mike nodded. "All right. I can be satisfied with that, I guess."

"And we'll just pretend that this day will go on and on, and there's nothing to worry about," she said, sniffing slightly. She wiped a tear from her eye and managed to smile. "How about some breakfast?"

He gave her a lopsided grin. "Well . . . okay." He held out his hand and she took it, and together they walked down the hill, into town.

Grace tried to concentrate on each step she took, on the calls of birds and the rustling of the leaves overhead. But as they passed under the shade of an elm she looked up into his face and felt a shadow of fear steal over her.

"Don't worry," he said, reading her thoughts.

She took a deep breath and nodded. "All right."

Hand in hand, they walked through the back streets of town and entered the garden of the Wild Rose Inn. At the gate, Grace stopped and twisted a blossom off the rosebush.

"I usually press one every summer for remembrance," she said. "But this time, I think I won't."

131

He took it from her, broke off the thorns, and then tucked it behind her ear. "It's perfect like that. It'll bloom all day."

Grace took another deep breath to keep the fear away. For now, she was determined to stay in the present, and be happy with that. "Stay here. I'll get us some coffee."

She went through the screen door into the house. The kitchen was empty, but someone, probably Rachel, had started coffee. As it percolated on the stove, Grace twitched the curtains aside to let the morning light spill across the checkerboard floor. Behind her, the door from the hallway opened and she turned with a blissful smile.

But it was Jimmy. Her smile froze as he came in, looking like a kicked dog.

"Grace," he said. "I didn't sleep at all last night, I felt so bad."

"Don't—"

"Just listen," he broke in. "I know I acted like a bastard, but give me another chance."

She shrank back in spite of herself, and seeing that, Jimmy winced. "Grace, please. We can start over, I know it. Just—please—" He broke off, turning away to hide his tears.

Grace stood helpless, unable to speak or help him at all. The memory of loving him was like a ghost, fading and insubstantial. She bowed her head in sorrow.

"Oh, God." Jimmy limped to the table and sat down, and put one hand over his eyes. "Grace, what happened to us?"

The screen door whined as it opened. Mike bounded in, and before Grace could speak, he caught her in his arms and swung her around. "I couldn't wait another—"

"Mike, no!" Grace cried.

He saw his friend. Grace let out a small gasp of dismay when she saw the expression on Jimmy's face.

"Jesus." Jimmy stood up abruptly, his chair skating backward. His eyes looked huge. "Jesus."

Mike turned from Grace to Jimmy. "Buddy, I'm—"

"Goddamn you!" Jimmy exploded. "Don't you 'buddy' me! You bastard, you stole my girl!"

"No, it wasn't like that," Grace said, her hands outstretched. "He never said a word until I told him I broke our engagement."

Jimmy didn't hear her. He was staring at Mike, trembling with anger and pain. Mike just shook his head and didn't try to make it better.

"All this time, you were sneaking behind my back," Jimmy spat out. "That is the most cowardly, disgusting behavior I've ever seen."

"He didn't do anything!" Grace insisted.

Jimmy turned on her with a look of loathing. "Nice work, Grace. You couldn't take a chance on damaged goods, right? But Mike's prime farm stock, a real healthy specimen. A war hero is nice, but not a crippled one."

Grace met his eyes squarely. "Don't do this, Jimmy, please. If you ever loved me, don't do this to yourself now."

He stared at her, incredulous. "Don't do this to *myself*? I think you've lost sight of the facts, Grace."

The hall door opened and Rachel came in, beaming with cheer. She stopped dead in her tracks when she saw the scene in front of her. "Pardon me, but . . ." She gestured helplessly toward the door.

Swearing, Jimmy barged past her and left the kitchen, limping hard. Rachel looked from Grace to Mike and back again.

"Oh, my God," Grace said, closing her eyes.

Mike swore under his breath, too. "I'll go talk to him."

"Mike, no!"

But he didn't listen to Grace. He ran by Rachel, and straight-armed through the swinging door after Jimmy.

The kitchen was very still, except for Grace's harsh breathing. Rachel came to Grace and folded her in her arms.

"Poor child," she murmured.

Grace put her head on Rachel's shoulder and stared dry-eyed at the coffeepot. She couldn't cry. She just couldn't cry.

That evening, Grace stood behind the bar as usual, pouring drinks and chitchatting with her out-of-town customers. But the regulars, the old-timers who came to the Wild Rose each night, kept their eyes down on their drinks and their answers brief. Grace felt the weight of their disappointment and disapproval wrap around her like a gloomy fog. In less than a day, it seemed, the whole town knew what had happened. She caught Mr. Staines's eye from across the room, and he looked reproachfully away. Grace wanted to pound her fists on the bar and tell them all that nobody could feel worse about what she had done to Jimmy than she did. But that was impossible.

And to make matters worse, every time the door opened, she prayed it would be Mike. Already, she was waiting for him to return, and there was nothing she could do about it. He hadn't even left for the war yet, but her heart was in her shoes.

"Mom, why did I have to be such an idiot?" she muttered as Mrs. MacKenzie joined her behind the bar. The jukebox was turned up too high, and people had to yell at one another to make themselves heard.

Her mother rang a check into the cash register. "What does that mean?"

"I'm so weak. I should have been stronger, but instead, I fell in love with a soldier again. Well, I'm not going to make that mistake again," she said in a low, vehement tone. "I'm not going to wait for Mike. I'm not going to tell him I love him, and I won't wait for him."

"Can I get a beer?" a man asked.

"In a minute," Mrs. MacKenzie replied, not even looking at him. She took Grace's arm and led her to the end of the bar, where it was more private. "Why do you say you won't wait for Mike? Do you love him or not?"

"Yes," Grace sighed. "Dammit, I do."

"Then don't be a fool. Don't waste another moment," her mother said. "Life is uncertain and precarious, especially during a war."

"Oh, miss?" the man called.

Mrs. MacKenzie whirled around. "Just a *moment*, sir."

Grace was beyond caring how her mother treated the patrons. She just hung her head.

"Now listen to me," Mrs. MacKenzie said. "You know I never felt any shame about getting pregnant before Bob and I got married. The only shame would have been not admitting the truth. I could never have married anyone else, so what difference did it make?"

"But Mom . . ."

The door from the lobby opened, and Mike stepped into the tavern. The hum of conversation died for a moment and then resumed. Grace and Mike looked at one another. Her heart yearned toward him.

"I said, can I get another beer, miss?" the tourist asked with obvious impatience.

Grace turned to wait on him, flustered with her work. When she turned around again, Mike was at the bar.

"I'm checking out," he said, his eyes on her.

"No—don't."

He jerked his head toward the door. "I'll stay in one of the boardinghouses, I guess. I get the feeling I'm not very welcome here."

"You are by me," she whispered.

While they gazed hopelessly into one another's eyes, Barbara came to the bar and perched on a stool. Startled, Grace looked at her friend.

Barbara tipped her head to one side, considering them. "People are talking," she began.

"I don't care what they say," Grace said passionately. "I don't care at all."

"Good for you." Barbara smiled at Grace's indignation. "Suddenly I'm seeing a whole new Grace."

Mike frowned, ready to defend Grace against any attack. "What are you saying?"

Laughing, Barbara put her hand over Mike's. "Relax. I'm all for it. See you tomorrow night."

She hopped off the bar stool and walked away, waving one hand at them over her shoulder.

"Is something happening tomorrow night?" Mike asked.

Grace put her head down on her hand and groaned. "The party."

Chapter Eleven

GRACE WAS TOO busy the next day to think about how miserable she was. Her hard work over the last two weeks had been too efficient: posters and handbills were up all over town announcing the dance and party, and it was impossible to cancel the event. The Wild Rose Inn would be packed that evening, no matter how much Grace wished she could hide herself away.

"The band Jimmy hired will be here at six-thirty," she told David, going over her checklist in the afternoon calm. She glanced around the kitchen table. "Sarah, can you make sure they get something to eat when they arrive?"

"I'll be awful busy," she warned.

Grace made herself give Sarah an encouraging smile. "But I know you can manage it perfectly, like you always do."

"Hmmph." Sarah stood up and went back to her

cake preparation, a flush of pride on her round face. Already, one cake was in the oven and adding a rich vanilla flavor to the air.

"Look how lovely this shines," Rachel commanded as she walked in from the pantry. She was holding the silver punch bowl, which gleamed like moonlight.

Grace felt her heart make a painful tug. Rachel put down the bowl in front of Grace, who stared at it, torn by uncertainty.

As long as they love each other and they're together, nothing else matters, Mike had said.

But they couldn't be together. There was no use denying it. He was going back to the war, and no matter how much she loved him, that wouldn't stop him from being killed, if that was his fate.

On the other hand she did love him, and she wanted to be with him, especially if their time was short.

"God, what a mess," she said out loud.

"No, it's not such a mess," David replied gloomily. "We can manage."

"I could use some help with these cakes, though," Sarah called over her shoulder. "One of 'em's ready to come out."

Nathan skipped into the kitchen, and Mrs. MacKenzie trailed in after him. "Darling, the liquor salesman is out front."

"Papa, I've got something to show you," Nathan said, tugging his father's sleeve.

Rachel put a cookie in his hand, turned him around

and gave him a gentle shove toward the door. "Not now, my pet. Go play, we're very very busy."

Pouting, Nathan whirled around at the door. "But it's only—"

"Not now, Nathan," Mrs. MacKenzie repeated. "Come to my room later, I'll give you an invisible bird."

"What is that?" the boy asked in amazement.

"I'll tell you later, now go." Hope pointed at the door.

Bright-eyed with excitement, Nathan ran out of the kitchen. "I'm going to have an invisible bird."

"Mom, you're terrible," Grace said with an embarrassed laugh.

Rachel and David both chuckled. "She's smart, your mother," Rachel told Grace. "You should do what she says."

Mrs. MacKenzie met Grace's eyes and gave her a challenging look. "Yes, Grace. You should follow my advice."

Everyone was looking at Grace. She felt as though she were being pulled in seventeen directions at once. The smell of sugary cake grew stronger and stronger.

"My hands are full!" Sarah warned in a loud voice. "The cake has to come out!"

"I'll just—" Grace began, flustered and jittery.

"Darling, the liquor man?" her mother said.

Grace held her hands out, as though trying to keep a crowd at bay. "All right. I'll deal with the liquor salesman, Rachel, can you help Sarah? And Mom, will you and David—"

"We know what to do," Mrs. MacKenzie said. "Go on."

Yanking off her apron, Grace hurried out of the kitchen to negotiate with the salesman. For the next two hours, she was so busy that she hardly had a moment to think. Extra help had been hired for the day, and Grace was run off her feet directing the placement of flowers, the hanging of streamers and bunting. She ordered the furniture in the tavern rearranged for more dancing, and then had to settle a dispute between the bandleader and the local traffic cop, who insisted the band couldn't park on Front Street to unload their instruments.

But even as she disposed of her problems one by one, Grace had one in the back of her mind she wasn't sure she could handle. As she paused in the lobby to catch her breath, she drummed her fingers on the telephone. On impulse, she snatched it up and dialed a familiar number.

"Hello?"

"Jimmy, it's me. Grace," she said quickly. "I just have to ask you, will you please come to the party tonight?"

He paused. Grace could picture him so well, sitting by the phone, his ankle crossed over his knee and the paper spread across his lap. Seconds ticked by.

"Please?" she whispered. "I care so much for you, even though you don't think so. We've been friends all our lives."

"It's amazing how little that counts, these days," he said bitterly.

Grace winced. "It counts for a lot, Jimmy. You know it does."

"Well, when a guy sees his best buddy steal his girl away—"

"Jimmy, listen," she broke in with a flash of anger. "I'm not a piece of jewelry, or a hundred dollar bill to be stolen. Mike didn't do anything."

He let out a soft, sardonic laugh. "Wow, that makes me feel even better. The guy does nothing at all, and he's still a better catch than I am."

"For the last time, it has nothing to do with Mike!" Grace said in an exasperated voice. "Right now, I'm talking about you and me, and all we've been through together. Please, Jimmy. Come to my party tonight. It would mean a lot to me."

She waited for him to answer. While the silence stretched, she watched the second hand on the lobby clock sweep a full circle, and nodded hello to two guests as they came in from the garden.

"Oh, okay, I'll come," Jimmy said at last. "Since it's your birthday party, and all."

Grace let out a sigh of relief, and even managed a small laugh. "It's not a birthday party, how many times do I have to say it?"

"I'll be there, Grace," he said in a softer tone. "I don't promise to have a good time, but I'll be there."

A tear came to her eye. "Thanks."

As she hung up the phone, someone called to her from the tavern, and she rushed off again, her mind racing.

Guests began to arrive at seven o'clock, and the tavern and dining room and parlors quickly filled. In spite of all Grace's protests, people had brought gifts for her, and the bar itself was soon covered with wrapped presents. Grace, surrounded by well-wishers, was too busy to worry about Jimmy, or wonder if her friends and neighbors were still disappointed by her decision. But in spite of the crush and the noise, she was always on the lookout for Mike. She had a horrible, sinking feeling that he wasn't going to show up, and in one moment of panic, she wondered if he had shipped out without saying good-bye.

"I've got to talk to you, Grace!" Barbara said, swooping down on her. She hooked her arm through Grace's and steered her away from the crowd and then continued in an undertone. "What's wrong, you're white as a sheet."

Grace sank gratefully into a chair in the corner. "Oh, I just lost my nerve for a minute, that's all," she said. She pressed her bottle of soda to her cheek, relishing the coolness, and from her corner she watched the festivities of the party. The band was good, and many couples were dancing. The older guests stood in small groups in animated conversation, and small children dodged through the crowd, shrieking with excitement.

"I called Jimmy today to make sure he would come," Grace told her friend.

Barbara made a face. "Ouch. Is he?"

"I don't know, I hope so," Grace said, gnawing on her thumbnail. "Or maybe not. I don't know anymore."

143

"I doubt he'd miss a chance to get some sympathy from the gang," Barbara said sourly.

Grace shook her head. "No, don't say that. And besides," she added in a low voice. "He deserves it."

"Don't start with that wounded hero line again," Barbara said. "Because I don't buy it. I don't believe a word of it, anyway."

"What are you saying?" Grace asked. She stared at her friend, appalled.

Barbara tossed her head, and took a sip of her Coke. "In my experience, people who accomplish brave and wonderful and heroic things don't go blabbing all over town about it. The ones who do that are generally fakes."

Grace stood up. "Barbie, give him a break. Don't try to take everything away from him."

"You're too nice, that's what you are," Barbara said with a sigh. She rose, too, and kissed Grace on the cheek. "Happy birthday, kiddo. And for what it's worth, you've got my blessing, you and Mike."

"We don't need it," Grace said awkwardly. "There's no 'we.'"

"Hmmph." Barbara shrugged and walked away.

Grace stayed where she was for a moment, unwilling to give up her peace and rejoin the party. She watched Rachel make her way through the crowd, and then Rachel caught Grace's eye and made a beeline for her.

"Grace, my Nathan. Have you seen him?" Rachel asked with a worried smile.

"No, I haven't," Grace said, glancing around at the crowd. She watched as some little girls in pink party dresses skipped by, and then frowned. "I haven't seen him since earlier this afternoon."

Rachel shook her head, and the expression on her face was a mixture of pride and exasperation. "That boy, what he gets up to."

"He'll show up soon, I'm sure," Grace said with another quick survey of the room.

"Yes, you are right, as always."

Rachel was beaming at Grace, but her expression fell. Grace followed the woman's gaze, and saw Mike and Jimmy, standing together at the bar. They were talking, but even from a distance, it was clear from their posture and gestures that both were tense and uncomfortable.

"Uh-oh," Rachel whispered.

Grace squared her shoulders and grabbed her soda. "I suppose I should do the brave thing and go over there."

Clucking her tongue, Rachel gave Grace a pat on the shoulder. "Go on, it won't be so bad. There are many harder things in this world."

Rachel's forthright sympathy made Grace love her even more. The hardships Rachel had been through dwarfed any problem that Grace had. She kissed Rachel's cheek and made her way to Mike's side.

"Well, hello," she said, not sure whom to look at.

Mike and Jimmy both straightened up when she joined them, and sent each other wary glances.

"Should I be drinking a toast to you two, now?" Jimmy asked, lifting a glass.

There was an awkward pause. Mike looked at question at Grace, but she felt the same crushing panic seize her again.

"Well?" Jimmy gave her a sardonic look.

"No," she blurted out.

Mike took a bottle of beer from the bar at his elbow. "How about we drink a toast to Vic? To fallen comrades."

"Fallen comrades," Jimmy repeated in a self-mocking tone. "That may be all of us, who can say?"

Grace raised her Coke bottle. "To Vic," she said, ignoring Jimmy's sarcasm.

In a silence so tense it was painful, the three drank to Vic, killed in the same assault that won Jimmy his medal. Grace felt as though her entire body vibrated like a wire, standing between Mike and Jimmy. She wanted so much to be with Mike, and yet couldn't bring herself to make any kind of promise to him. Standing on her other side was the painful reminder that such promises could be impossible to keep. Too awkward and uncomfortable to speak, the three of them turned to the front of the room as the band started up a waltz.

"May I have this dance?"

Grace turned to David with a grateful smile. "Thank you for rescuing me," she said as he waltzed her away. On the dance floor, mostly older couples turned and glided to the old-fashioned music.

David looked at her gravely. "It is very sad, but a woman must follow her heart. A woman is naturally weaker than a man."

"David, I don't believe that's true, and what's more, I don't think you believe it yourself," Grace said with a shocked laugh. "Look at all the jobs women have been doing during this war. Isn't that evidence that women are just as strong?"

He shrugged and said no more. Grace frowned, wondering what to make of his comment. She knew she was following her heart by turning down Jimmy. But was she strong enough to follow her heart all the way?

She glanced back at the bar. Jimmy and Mike had both disappeared.

"David," Rachel interrupted. "David, have you seen Nathan?"

David and Grace stopped in the middle of the dance floor. David patted his wife's hand. "You are worrying without reason, Rachel. You always spoil the boy."

Grace put one hand to her cheek. She was hot and flushed, either from dancing or from the discomfort of her thoughts. As she stood catching her breath, she pictured Nathan's excited face as he played soldiers on the cliffs.

"I need some fresh air," she said to the Teitelbaums. "I'll take a look for Nathan outside."

"Oh, I never looked outside," Rachel said, slapping her forehead in disgust. "What a fool."

"He's probably just playing with some of the other children in the garden," Grace suggested. "You two stay and make sure the party runs the way it should."

Before they could answer her, Grace slipped through the crowd and let herself out of the tavern into the twilight.

147

Chapter Twelve

GRACE SHRUGGED INTO a light jacket as she hurried along the street. The sound of music faded behind her and the Wild Rose Inn receded into the dusk. She called Nathan's name, but did not expect an answer. She hurried on, her mind spinning, and caught sight—through a lighted window—of an old woman standing alone, drinking a glass of wine. Grace put her head down.

Sand kicked up from her heels and sprinkled her bare calves as she ran along the shoulder of the road. The sky above was still luminous with the sunset, and the breeze off the water filled her ears with a hushed roar. The smell of the rising tide was pungent and sharp, the smell of dead fish and brine and the rolling ocean. She knew it was sucking and grabbing at the base of the cliffs that dropped away from the edge of the road. The promontory where Nathan had shouted his small defiance was just ahead. She could see its black shoulders hunched against the graying sky.

As she drew nearer to the cliffs, the silhouette of a man emerged from the surrounding shadows: one man, sitting on the edge of the cliff, facing the Atlantic.

"Hello!" Grace called. "Have you seen a little boy playing here?"

The man didn't reply. Grace jogged a few more steps, and recognized him with a shock. It was Jimmy.

"Jimmy?" She faltered on the path and then continued. Even as she approached, her heels tapping loudly on the rocks, he didn't turn around. With growing confusion and a vague sense of alarm, Grace walked to his side and looked down.

His face was wet: his cheeks, his brow, his lips. His eyes were shut tight and he held onto the rocks at his sides with the rigid grip of a man who sees the world ending before him. Grace felt her whole soul turn over in horror and fear.

"What's wrong?" she gasped, kneeling beside him. She put her hand on his arm. It was as hard and unmoving as iron. "What happened?"

"Don't do it," he whispered through clenched teeth. "Don't do it. We'll never make it, Vic."

"*What?*" Grace asked, her eyes wide.

"It's too dangerous, stay here," he said. He was shaking, and the sweat stood out on his face as if he was in terror of his life.

Grace looked around wildly. "Vic is dead, Jimmy,"

she said, her heart cold and sick with pity. "What are you saying?"

The wind buffeted them, and Grace had to clutch the rock to brace herself. A sound reached her, blown up on the wind from somewhere over the cliffs. Her heart pounding, she inched away from Jimmy and looked over.

Fifteen feet below her, Mike stood pressed against the cliff, shielding Nathan with his body. The tide foamed white just a foot below him. Grace felt dizzy as she stared down at them.

"Mike! Mike!"

He looked up, his face pale in the fading light. "The boy's hurt! I can't carry him and climb up at the same time!" he shouted over the wind and the dull crash of the waves.

Grace squeezed her eyes shut, and then jerked around sharply. She couldn't understand why Jimmy was just sitting there, motionless. "Jimmy! Why don't you help?"

He seemed incapable of answering, lost in some horrifying dream of the war. His lips moved in a constant, desperate whisper of "Vic, don't, Vic, don't." Grace crawled to the edge of the cliff again.

"What's wrong with Jimmy?" she cried, her eyes stinging with salt spray and tears.

Mike was holding Nathan now, and the boy had his arms wrapped tight around Mike's neck. "He froze!" Mike yelled. "He froze when Vic got killed and he's frozen now. He can't help! He can't do anything! Go get help!" A wave flung itself up over the ledge Mike stood on, washing over his feet and falling back.

For a moment Grace was too stunned by Mike's words to move. Jimmy had frozen on the beach at Normandy. He had watched a man under his command killed, and he had lost control of his fear. He wasn't a hero at all, and Mike had been protecting him ever since the invasion. She turned to stare at Jimmy, and then, with a cry of physical pain, Grace put one hand over her eyes.

"Grace! Grace!"

Mike's shouts snapped her to attention, and she dragged herself to look over the cliff again, roughly wiping the tears from her eyes. The sight of the water reaching up to Mike and Nathan filled her with dread. She swallowed hard.

"I'm coming down!"

"No, go get help!" Mike waved her back, but Grace ignored him. She swung her legs down over the edge, and felt for a foothold. Her heart pounding, she began to lower herself down the face of the cliff. She kept her eyes on Jimmy's rigid form at the top, praying for him to pull himself out of his panic and trying to deafen herself to the sound of the waves against the rocks below.

"Grace, go back!" Mike shouted.

Carefully, slowly, she turned herself around on a ledge above him. "There's no time," she explained, meeting his eyes with an anguished look. Nathan was whimpering, his face buried in Mike's neck. Grace shook her head. "What happened?"

"Jimmy and I came out here for a walk," Mike explained, one wary eye on the water at his feet. "We saw Nathan, and saw him go over. Jimmy wanted us to go back to the Wild Rose for help, but I told him I could get the kid."

A gust of wind sprayed Grace with brine. She shook her damp hair out of her eyes and looked back up the cliff. The light was fading fast, but she could see Jimmy. He was leaning farther out over the edge, watching them.

"Jimmy!" she screamed. "Can you hear me?"

He didn't move. She couldn't even tell if his eyes were on her, and if they were, what he saw.

"Please," she whispered, staring up at him. "Please go."

Jimmy's head jerked back from view, and he was gone. But whether he was still there or whether he had gone for help, she had no idea. Grace felt her stomach plunge, and she gripped the cliff face, grating her fingernails against the damp rock.

A wave crashed against the ledge where Mike and Nathan stood, and Grace heard Nathan let out a wail of fear. Then Mike murmured a kind word of encouragement to the boy, and Grace felt it give her courage, too. She turned around, struggling out of her jacket.

"I'll help you," she called, kneeling down and twisting the jacket into a rope. She smiled at Nathan, who stared at her and then hid his face against Mike's shoulder. The legs of Mike's pants were soaking wet, and drops wet his arms and his hair and face. Grace met his eyes.

"I'm not going to let you die right here in Marblehead," she said harshly.

"I'm not going to let me die, either."

Grace felt a sob catch in her throat, but she made herself choke it down. She forced herself to smile easily for the little boy's sake.

"Nathan, can you reach this?" she called in a cheerful voice. "See if you can grab onto my jacket! I know you're a strong boy!"

Whimpering, Nathan looked up, his eyes wide. He shuddered as another wave surged up around Mike's legs.

"Just hold onto the jacket and I'll push you," Mike said. "Grace will pull you up where she's standing. Do you see how easy that will be?"

Grace and Mike shared another look. It wouldn't be easy at all, not unless Nathan could help himself. She lay down on her stomach, ignoring the sharp points of granite that dug in between her ribs. In the failing light, the twisted rope of her jacket was like a banner.

"Just grab that, Nathan. We're missing the party! And all your friends are there," she coaxed. Her pulse was racing so fast she could hardly breathe, but she kept her gaze steady on Nathan's. Mike stretched as high as he could and caught the end of the jacket and boosted the child up onto his shoulder.

"Go on," Mike said. "You can do it."

The boy reached out one hand, and then the other, and gripped the jacket tight. Mike shifted him again, lifting him up as high as he could. Grace's heart was in her mouth.

"Hold on tight, Nathan," she said. "I've got you."

She pulled up, her shoulders straining, and never took her eyes off of Nathan's. One of his legs was injured, but he scrabbled for a foothold with the other and came scrambling up the side of the cliff to Grace. She released one of her hands from the rope and grabbed his shirt, and dragged him up and into her lap. He clung to her, his arms so tight around her neck she was afraid he would strangle her.

"I didn't mean to fall," he said in a tiny voice.

"I know, darling," she said, stroking his hair and holding him close. "I know. Now sit right here while I help Mike."

She looked over the edge again. Mike had inched himself back as far as he could, hugging the wall. Water foamed around his knees and sucked at his feet. He stared up at Grace and managed to smile.

"Any time you want to give me a hand, I'd be much obliged."

With a shaky smile, Grace let the twisted jacket dangle over the edge again. Mike caught it in both hands. "Are you sure you can hold on?" he asked with an uncertain look.

Grace nodded, although she wasn't at all sure. "Of course. Just hurry."

He nodded, and then put all his weight against the line. Grace took such a jolt in her shoulders that she thought they'd been dislocated. But in just a moment, he had kicked one long leg over the ledge and rolled up beside her and Nathan. They put their arms around one another, panting, and held each other tight. Mike was wet and shivering, and the waves flung drops of water up to where they huddled.

"This won't be safe long," Grace said. "We have to keep going up."

Nathan let out a wail. "Mama!"

"She'll be here in a moment," Grace promised, gathering the child into her arms.

She cast a frightened look at Mike. Neither of them could be certain help was on the way. He put one hand over hers.

"Promise me one thing," he asked in a calm voice.

"Anything," Grace told him.

"If we get out of this, you'll marry me."

Grace felt another sob rise in her throat. "Yes," she whispered. "Damn you, I will."

They stared at each other for a long moment, and suddenly, the end of a rope dropped down between them. It dangled and quivered. They stared at it in speechless amazement, and then both let out screams of wild, jubilant laughter.

"We're here!" Mike shouted up the cliff.

"He did it," Grace whispered. "Thank God."

At the top, a crowd of people milled around, yelling orders and lowering ropes. Still laughing from sheer relief, Mike tied the first rope around Grace, under her arms.

"It'll hurt like hell, but it'll get you up," he warned. He handed Nathan to her, and the boy wrapped his arms tightly around her neck.

"Hang on, sweetie," Grace said in his ear. "We're being rescued, now."

"Take her up!" Mike shouted, giving a tug on the rope.

Grace never took her eyes off Mike as she was hoisted up and away from their rocky ledge. He was almost swallowed by the darkness, but she could feel him watching her, too. And then, arms reached out for her, and took Nathan and helped her onto the ground.

Everyone from the Wild Rose was there, Rachel and David crying over their child, Hope and Barbara fussing around Grace. And Jimmy, standing in the midst of the crowd, watching her with pain in his eyes.

"Once a hero, always a hero," Mr. Denunzio said loudly. "Even with a bum leg, he hightailed it back here to save these young peoples' lives."

All eyes turned to Jimmy, many filled with tears of gratitude and admiration. He kept looking at Grace, unable to speak. Grace waited, and her heart broke for him.

"Heave! Up we go!" the men at the cliff yelled.

With a wild scramble, Mike was up and over the edge of the cliff. He stayed on hands and knees for a moment, panting, while the rescue gang surrounded him and wrapped him in blankets. Grace shivered.

Stiffly, Jimmy walked toward Mike. The crowd fell silent as the two regarded one another. Grace was torn between wanting to protect Jimmy, and wanting Mike to get the credit he deserved. He was the true hero, and no one knew it but her.

"Thank your lucky stars Jimmy saw what happened to you folks," Mrs. Penworthy said at last.

Grace stepped forward and bit back a cry. She turned pleading eyes to Jimmy. Tears began to run down his face.

"I never did anything," he said in a choking voice. "I never did what they say I did. It was Mike all along. It was him."

"No, what are you saying!" Mr. Pitney exclaimed. "You're overexcited, that's understan—"

"No!" Jimmy wiped the tears from his cheeks. "I'm no hero, and it's because of me that Vic died. I don't deserve your respect, or your love. And I sure don't deserve Grace MacKenzie."

His painful, wracking sobs were shocking to hear in the stunned silence. Jimmy stood alone at the center of the crowd, until Mike pulled himself to his feet and went to his friend.

"Hey, let's take it easy now, Jim," Mike said as he put one arm across Jimmy's heaving shoulders. "How about I take you home? I guess you're a little worn out."

Suddenly, the unseen hand that had kept everyone back pulled away. Mrs. Penworthy and a circle of friends surrounded Jimmy and led him away. Mike stood watching them go, and Grace watched him, so proud and in love that she thought she wouldn't survive the force of her emotion.

"Holy crow," Barbara whispered. "Maybe I oughtta change my mind about what my type of guy is."

Grace laughed, a nearly hysterical sound, and turned

to her friend. "Oh, no you don't," she said in a firm voice. "He's mine."

Mike came to Grace and took her in his arms. "You're stuck with me, whether you want me or not. Remember, you promised to marry me if we got out of that fix."

"You did?" Barbara gasped.

Blushing, Grace tucked her arm through Mike's. "You make all kinds of crazy promises when you're standing on a ledge with the tide rising."

"But this one I'm holding you to," he swore.

The crowd began to move as a body back toward town, and now that the danger was past, everyone began talking at once about Mike and Grace's daring rescue of Nathan. Rachel was sobbing and laughing by turns as David bore the little boy to the Wild Rose, and everyone poured into the inn to resume the party.

On the threshhold Grace paused with Mike's arm around her, and looked at the tavern as though seeing it for the first time. The streamers and bunting moved in the drafts of air the crowd made as it moved, and the pile of birthday gifts on the bar was like a mountain of good cheer.

"I'm so happy to be home," she said, smiling blissfully at Mike.

"So am I," he said.

Grace let out a sigh of happiness and put her head on his shoulder.

"So how about it?" Mike asked her.

She looked up. Her mother and Barbara were standing nearby, and they both looked keenly at Mike, as though urging him on. The band began playing again, and couples began to take over the dance floor.

"How about what?" Grace asked.

Mike was grinning from ear to ear. "Let's get married. Right now."

"*Now?*" Grace's voice rose in a squeak.

Hope began to laugh. "My very proper, cautious, by-the-book daughter."

"You've already got the party and the gifts," Barbara pointed out with a giggle. "And the minister's here, too. He's having a beer with Mr. Pitney."

Wide-eyed, Grace looked from Barbara, to her mother, to Mike, and shook her head in astonishment. "Are you serious?"

Mike grabbed her in his arms and swung her around. "Don't you know there's a war on?" he asked.

"But I—" Grace gaped at them, and then gestured to her blue and white flowered dress. "But I'm not—"

"You look beautiful in that dress," Barbara insisted. "And you're only a tiny bit wind-blown. Go on. Get married. I'll get Reverend Potter."

"But . . ." Grace was flabbergasted. She kept looking at Mike and her mother and back again.

"Maybe you don't want to marry her," Mrs. MacKenzie told Mike dryly. "She has lost the power of speech."

"As long as she can say 'I do,' " Mike said with a laugh.

Grace's pulse was racing so fast she thought she would faint. She had never considered anything so rash and unplanned in her life, let alone something so important. Her mother caressed her cheek and bent close to her ear.

"Would you give your life for him?" Hope asked.

Grace pictured the ledge on the cliffs, and as she met Mike's twinkling eyes, every last doubt finally vanished.

"Absolutely."

"Then what are you waiting for?" Hope asked, arching her dark brows.

Grace began to laugh. Mike took her hand and squeezed it.

"Attention, can I have your attention?" Barbara grabbed the microphone from the bandleader and shushed the band. She grinned at the crowd. "I have an important announcement to make. The Reverend Mr. Potter would like to perform a certain ceremony."

Startled murmurs raced through the crowd. People jostled and craned their heads to see, and then parted as Mr. Potter walked up to Grace and Mike. Grace blushed with happiness and excitement, and Mr. Potter bent a kindly gaze on them both.

"You can formalize this tomorrow with a license," he whispered. "But I'd love to marry you right now."

Grace and Mike grinned at each other. The crowd whispered and gasped, and there was a smattering of applause.

"They make a lovely couple," an old woman said in a loud voice.

It was like being in a dream, Grace thought, but every bit of it was true. She was holding Mike's hand, and Mr. Potter was repeating the words of the marriage cere-

160

mony, and everyone she loved, except for her father and brother, was there and happy and wishing her happiness. Mike solemnly vowed to love and cherish her until death, and Grace felt as though she could take flight. Beaming, Mr. Potter turned to her.

"And do you, Grace Ann Carter MacKenzie, take Michael Holmquist to be your husband, to love and cherish above all others, until death do you part?"

Mike looked steadily into her eyes. Grace found herself nodding, and a smile spreading across her face. "I do," she said in a loud, clear voice.

The tavern of the Wild Rose Inn was as quiet and hushed as a church. Even the children were still in the face of such a solemn moment. Grace met Mike's eyes and knew that no matter what came, no matter what the war would bring, their love would outlast everything.

Mr. Potter tucked in his chin with a benevolent smile. "Well? Go ahead," he said to Mike. "You may now kiss the bride."

Both Grace and Mike laughed.

"You wouldn't think they needed reminding," Barbara said loudly. She popped a champagne cork. "To happy days!" she toasted as the bottle bubbled over.

"Happy days!" the crowd echoed.

Mike and Grace kissed, and the Wild Rose Inn resounded with cheers.

Follow the sweeping saga of generations
of young MacKenzie women, all growing up
at the Wild Rose Inn.

BRIDIE OF THE WILD ROSE INN
1695

Sixteen-year-old Bridie MacKenzie has waited ten years in Scotland to join her parents in the Massachusetts Bay Colony. Bridie's happiness at being reunited with her family is tempered by the reality of her new life. Her loving parents work day and night to make ends meet at their small, rough inn, and they have had to give up their religion for Puritanism under the colony's law.

Spirited Bridie refuses to conform to the rules—she vows not to give up either her faith or the healing herbs she has brought from Scotland. But all that Bridie believes in, the Puritans denounce as witchcraft. The price of holding on to her convictions may be high. Must Bridie lose her new home, her reputation, and her first true love for what she believes?

ANN OF THE WILD ROSE INN
1774

The dangers are terrifying for Ann MacKenzie and her twin brother, John, but both of them are willing to involve themselves in smuggling and other risky activities—anything to help their struggling country.

Marblehead, home to the Wild Rose Inn that's been in Ann's family since they first came to America nearly one hundred years ago, is no longer the tranquil place it once was. Tensions have increased between England and the colonies, and the locals resent the presence of the British military.

Ann does, too, until she falls in love with a handsome, sensitive young man she meets along the shore—a stranger who turns out to be a British sailor. Loving the enemy is wrong, but Ann can't help herself. Where should her allegiance lie? With her family and country, or with the love of her life?

EMILY OF THE WILD ROSE INN
1858

Emily MacKenzie is content spending her days sailing and working at the Wild Rose Inn with Lucy, her best friend and adopted sister. The rift between the North and South is growing, but Emily has never given much thought to the troubling social issues of the day, nor to the dangerous work of the Underground Railroad in her own town.

But conflict ensnares Emily when the Stockwells, a wealthy southern family, come to stay at the Inn with their slave, Moses. Emily knows in her heart that slavery is wrong, and wishes she could help Moses. But her growing feelings for Blount, the Stockwells' son, hold her back. By helping Moses, she would betray Blount, but taking Blount's side would compromise her values and destroy her heartfelt friendship with Lucy, a free black. Can Emily find the strength to do what must be done?

LAURA OF THE WILD ROSE INN
1898

On the eve of the twentieth century, the world is changing rapidly, and sixteen-year-old Laura MacKenzie wants to be a part of the coming age. Her parents, forever entrenched in their old-fashioned ways, are running the Wild Rose Inn the same way their family has for two centuries. Laura is sure there must be more to life than she finds in rustic Marblehead, Massachusetts, if only she were given the chance to leave and seek her destiny for herself.

When Laura meets Grant Van Doren, a student at Yale, she's introduced to new possibilities. Laura can almost taste the freedom and adventures Grant and the new era offer her. Under Grant's spell, all seems possible. Can Laura depend on Grant and his promises, or is her future something she must find for herself?

CLAIRE OF THE WILD ROSE INN
1928

Since her father's death, hardworking Claire MacKenzie has kept afloat the Wild Rose Inn, her family's business for generations. But now that Prohibition has made liquor illegal, the Wild Rose cannot compete with the speakeasies that peddle bootleg alcohol. Claire's brother, Bob, wants to make the Wild Rose a speakeasy, but Claire doesn't want to be involved in any crime—including bootlegging.

Then Claire finds the town drunk shot dead on his boat, and she is drawn into a criminal world. Police Chief Handy inexplicably dismisses the case, but determined, curious Claire wants answers. Her only ally is Hank Logan, a newspaper reporter looking for a scoop. Together they investigate, and every lead brings Claire closer to Hank—and home. It looks as if her brother's efforts to save the inn have gotten him mixed up with gangsters. Claire has learned things are not always what they seem. Whom can she really trust? Will Claire risk her family, the Wild Rose Inn, and her new love for Hank to get to the dangerous truth?

ABOUT THE AUTHOR

Jennifer Armstrong is the author of many books for children and young adults, including the historical novel *Steal Away*, the Pets, Inc., series, and several picture books.

Jennifer Armstrong lives in Saratoga Springs, New York, in a house more than 150 years old that is reputed to have been a tavern. In addition to writing, she raises guide-dog puppies and works in her garden, where roses grow around the garden gate.